Previous Books in
The Unspoken Series
by Marilyn Grey

Book #1

Where Love Finds You
Ella & Matthew

Book #2

Down from the Clouds
Gavin

the *life* I now live

MARILYN GREY

WINSLET PRESS

The Life I Now Live
Copyright © 2013 by Marilyn Grey

To learn more about Marilyn Grey, visit her Web site:
www.marilyn-grey.com

Library of Congress Control Number: 2013951090

ISBN-10: 0985723521
ISBN-13: 978-0985723521

Cover & Interior Design by Tekeme Studios

Printed in the United States of America

First Edition: November 2013
13   12   11   10   9   8   7   6   5   4   3   2   1

To:
Laura Dobb

For:
being a fun & amazing fan
of The Unspoken Series

*The heart has its reasons which
reason knows not.*
Blaise Pascal

*We must be willing to let go of
the life we have planned, so as to have
the life that is waiting for us.*
E. M. Forster

*I hold it true, whate'er befall;
I feel it, when I sorrow most;
'Tis better to have loved and lost
Than never to have loved at all.*

Alfred Lord Tennyson

Chapter One
Heidi

Snowflakes piled up on each other as I rocked Riley to sleep. The ground turned white as I thought of the things I kept hidden. The rings on my left hand sparkled in the glow of a candle, reminding me of the lies. I tried to convince myself that a secret is only a lie if it harms someone. For so long my secrets only harmed myself. Now, sweet Patrick introduced himself to my life and pretended to not fall in love with me. And my secrets would harm him if he got too close. So I built a wall between us to keep him from the truth. The heartbreak.

I called him my best friend. Nothing more. He accepted that. He accepted everything. Sometimes I wished he weren't so nice. Sometimes I wished he would pry the truth out of me and set me free. But he didn't know. No one did. My lies were so real that I grew to believe them myself.

Snowflakes pressed against the window. I placed Riley in her crib, on her side like she liked. Her eyes flickered and then closed. I longed for the kind of peace she had. Soon life would steal it from her too. A life of many painful surgeries and nights in the hospital. A life without her father.

I laid my cheek against the cold window. Inhaled.

"You can do this," I whispered to myself.

My cell phone vibrated in my pocket. A text from Ella.

I ignored it.

I loved Gavin and Ella. Who wouldn't? Most loving people I'd ever known. But that's not all. They were also the happiest and most gorgeous couple I'd ever known. I know they had their histories too. We all do. But they handled everything so well. Together. They were everything I ever wanted and nothing I ever had. They were beautiful. And if you looked under the delicate mounds of snow on my heart you wouldn't find beauty.

The sheet of white hid a landfill of lost hopes and dreams. Brokenness.

I often wondered if I'd ever be able to start over. Start a new life with Patrick. A life so different from anything I'd ever known.

I tiptoed across the room, closed the door, and walked downstairs. Patrick must've cleaned the kitchen for me. Again. Something Andy never had enough time or energy to do for me. Not since his promotion. The one that sucked the life from our marriage.

I grabbed a bottle of water and sat on the couch. Patrick's shoes were still on the floor by the door. He must've stayed.

I peeked outside. The wind blew snow on my face. I breathed in the winter air and shut the door.

"Hey," Patrick said. Voice quiet, eyes concerned.

"I can't believe you waited so long. I thought you left."

"That was the plan, but something isn't right with you tonight. I didn't want to leave you here alone."

"I'm okay."

"You're not okay."

I wanted to tell him the truth. Tell him what he was getting himself into. Instead, I touched his hand, lingered there for a second, and walked away. Back to the couch.

"Okay," he said from behind me. "I am just going to be a straight up with you."

I waited. Looked down at my stomach. The stomach that once held another life. A life that wouldn't be here if it weren't for Andy and our love.

"Are you listening?" he said. "Heidi, I need you to look at me."

He knelt down on the floor beside me. Took my hand.

I jerked. "No, Pat. I can't."

He looked at his hand, then laughed. "I look like I'm about to propose, huh?"

I nodded. Confused.

"I just knelt here. Didn't mean to scare you." He half-smiled and sat beside me. "I'm not proposing until your hand is free to accept the ring."

It sounded like he already had the ring. My stomach turned as my my heart fought between excitement and anxiety. I know it seemed crazy to most people around me, but I was still married. Andrew Chase was dead to the world. His ashes spread across the hills of America. To me, though, he was still alive. The echoes of his heart still beating to the rhythm of my own heart.

Ella thought of me as admirable. She never said a word, but I knew she didn't approve of Patrick. She wanted us to stay faithful to our dead spouses. Her idealism could choke the life out of any normal person if she let it. Most people can't live like that. Sure, it's ideal, but not easy. If only she knew why I wanted to stay faithful, maybe then she'd realize I'm not as romantic as I seem. Just scared. Scared and alone.

"What's wrong?" Patrick said as I wiped my eyes.

I shook my head and reclined on the couch. Patrick sat at my feet, afraid to touch me, but I could tell he wanted to.

"Look," he said, eyes ahead. I couldn't help but notice his defined jaw and the muscles in his neck. "I didn't want to say this, but I love you Heidi. I love what we have. I love who I am when I'm with you. I love you." He exhaled and looked at me. "There. I said it."

I looked down, trying to hide the tears. I wanted him so much. I wanted to wrap my arms around his neck and let him love me. I wanted to run away from the past and start a new life with him. But what I wanted didn't matter. I needed to stay faithful to Andy. I had no choice.

I promised. And I feared breaking this promise. Not because I'm a wonderful person. Because I would always live my life wondering "what if" and what could've been. That wouldn't be fair to Patrick.

I reached for his hand. My heart tearing at the edges, but staying in tact. I loved him. I really did. But never in a million years could I tell him. Allowing Patrick into my heart meant saying goodbye to Andrew. Forever. My Andy. My first love.

I twirled the rings on my finger and looked at Patrick. "I know you love me. I know our friendship is special. I appreciate you a—"

"You appreciate me a lot, but you don't love me. You still love Andy."

I nodded, tears fending for life on my lashes. I blinked and watered my cheeks. "Life doesn't make sense, Pat."

"It makes perfect sense," he said. "I married a girl I loved more than my own life, and she happened to love her own life more than she loved me. It would only make sense that I'd fall for a woman who loved another man

13

more than she could ever love me."

I watched him speak. He continued pouring his heart into my hands as I focused on his lips. He was more attractive than Andy. Than any guy I'd ever been with. Short chocolatey hair. Eyes the color of the Atlantic Ocean. Fit, but still looked cuddly.

He kept talking. I couldn't focus on his words. Not with his rolled up sleeves highlighting his wrists and hands. It had been so long since I'd been with a man. Felt the warmth of a man's touch on my skin in a way only lovers embrace.

I shoved the thoughts into a mental drawer and locked it.

"Pat." I stood. "I want you to know that I care about you a lot. I really do. I know you've had a difficult past. I have too. But I need to do this. Please, trust me when I say it's not you. You are amazing. It's me. It's all me."

He stood. Inches from my face. My lips silently begged him to come closer, but I couldn't. I stepped back. Looked down and caught my breath.

"I need to get some rest," I said. "We'll talk tomorrow."

He kissed my hand, respectfully, tipped his hat, and walked out of my house. I watched his car drive out of sight and broke down on the living room floor. I hated what my life had become. I hated that the only lovers I had known were Andy and my tears. One gone, the other unwanted. And I hated that a gorgeous man with an even more amazing heart wanted to lead me to a better life. A life I desperately wanted my entire life, but it was too late. I already sent my heart to someone else, self-addressed stamped envelope not included. I couldn't get it back. Even if I wanted to.

Chapter Two
Patrick

When I woke to my phone beeping at 3:17am my heart raced, hoping I'd see her middle of the night declaration of love for me.

I rubbed my eyes and read her text.

You awake?

Yes, I responded.

A few minutes passed. I turned on the light and sat up. No response. I texted again. *Everything okay?*

Sorry. Riley woke up. I can't sleep. I have this weird nightmare sometimes. It's been happening a lot lately. Can you come over?

I didn't hesitate. Yes, I had to work the next day, but somehow you need less sleep when you're in love.

I parked in front of her house sixteen minutes later, unlocked the door, and looked around. Every room downstairs was lit up. No sign of her. I went upstairs and knocked on her door. Nothing. Peeked in Riley's room and saw them both asleep in the rocking chair. I lifted the baby and put her in the crib, covered her in a pink blanket, and walked back to Heidi. Still flopped over asleep in the chair. I picked her up and carried her to her bedroom, laid her head on the pillow, and pulled the sheets up to her neck. She curled onto her side and smiled.

"I'm here if you need me," I whispered, then grabbed a pillow and a fleece blanket from the closet.

After one more look at her sleeping face I made myself comfortable, or as comfortable as I could, on the floor beside her bed. I bet it wasn't more than an hour when I woke to a bang and a high pitch scream.

I jumped up and looked around the room. Heidi stared at me, in a daze.

"What just happened?" I said.

She flopped backwards onto the pillows. "These dreams. I keep having these dreams that someone is after me."

"No one is after you."

"I don't feel safe here." She closed her eyes. "I've never lived alone before, and now that I have a baby to protect I feel even more paranoid."

"I can understand that," I said. "But there's nothing to be afraid of."

"What if you bought the house across the street? It's been on the market for a year."

"I can't. I'm already paying for my apartment plus helping you out with this mortgage. There's no way I could pay for two mortgages at once."

"What if you moved in with me? You could fix the basement up and live there."

I chewed the inside of my cheek and considered the possibility. "I don't know. Might be weird for Riley. She'd grow up thinking of me as her uncle and that's not what I want to be."

Her eyes opened. She turned her body toward me. I stood there. Arms at my sides. Wanting to hold her. To be hers.

"What do you want to be?" she said, a hint of flirtation in her voice.

"Don't play with me," I said. "You know what I want. It's not a game, Heidi. We're not in middle school. This isn't a check yes or no if you like me game. I love you, okay? What more can I say? I want to be with you. If that means I'm your best friend until the day I die, then okay. I can deal with that. But you know what I want."

She sat up. "Why, Pat? Tell me why. How can you love me? We barely know each other."

"Not true." I sat beside her. "You know me well and I know you as well as anyone can. You don't let many people in right now. I think I'm as close to you as someone can get."

"But what about me do you love?" She wasn't playing. She was serious. "And don't say everything."

"There's not just a list of qualities, although I could give you plenty of those. It's us. What we have. I love what you and me equal."

She thought for a moment, then said, "What about Gavin and Ella?"

"What about them?"

16

"You think we have something like them?"

I laughed. "No one does. That's their own thing. Ella creates love stories wherever she goes. You're not Ella. I'm not Gavin. But that doesn't mean that what we have is anything less special. It's just us. It's the picture you see when the puzzle pieces find their match. I like this picture."

She reached for my hand. Squeezed, then let go. "It's more complicated than that."

"It's not. You're just making it that way."

"You don't understand. There's more to the story, but I'm not allowed to say anything."

"Says who?"

"I can't say."

MAN, IT KILLED ME TO WALK AWAY FROM HER. I NEVER imagined falling in love again. Not after the hell on earth I endured with Emily. When she died I told myself no woman would ever be worth that again. You spend your life fighting for a girl only to have her give up and die, and that was before the cancer killed her. It certainly doesn't make you want to fight again.

Maybe this sounds bad, I don't know and I really don't care, but I wanted to be fought for too. Not in a damsel in distress kind I way. I was no damsel and I wasn't quite distressed. Yet.

I wanted to be loved. Really loved. Like my friends. Gavin and Matt. Their wives smiled at them from across the room with such sweetness. Lydia went through a lot as she waited for Matt to choose her. She fought. She gave up something.

Why did I fall for women who were locked behind walls with no windows? Heidi was different than Emily. She didn't seem as depressed. Just sad. And the chemistry between us. She hid from it, but there's no mistaking those kind of sparks. Still. She stood behind an enormous brick wall and I wasn't sure I had the energy to chip at the bricks.

If only I had a grenade, I thought. That would work.

I walked into my apartment, took my shoes off, and immediately got into bed. Midnight. About the time I always went to bed now that I spent most nights with Heidi.

Her face lived in my mind. A permanent resident. I closed my eyes and saw her. Tears running down her face. I wanted to know her. To get behind the wall and find out what she really felt.

She made it so difficult. Looking down and seeing that ring on her finger didn't help. I loved her. Wanted her so bad it hurt. But not with that ring on her finger.

I pulled the sheets over my head, rolled to my side, and wondered how life became so twisted. On my nightstand, my own wedding band reflected the red light from the alarm clock beside it. Emily. She would've been sleeping in the bed right now. Me, on the couch. Never allowed to touch her. If I tried to hold her hand, she flinched. She blamed it on her past. I had no doubt. Being raped by your dad when you're seven years old would mess me up too. But doesn't there come a time when you need to bury the past? When you stop using it as excuse to curl up in a ball and not live your life? Doesn't there come a time when the past no longer lives in the present and muddies the future?

I was tired of mud. So exasperated with it. I flung the covers off, grabbed the ring, opened my window, and flung it out into the winter wonderland. Shivering, I jumped back into bed and smiled. The past one step closer to really, truly, being behind me.

Heidi's face appeared again. Bright eyes and wavy hair just past her shoulders. The way she smiled at me. She loved me. I knew she did. If only she'd admit it and let the bricks fall to the ground.

I wanted to fight for her, albeit tired. But I feared the grenade didn't exist on my side of the wall. She held it. Firmly. Right there on her left hand ring finger.

Oh well, I thought as I picked up my phone and texted her.

I love you.

Take it or leave it, I decided to love her whether she loved me or not. Not like I could help it anyway.

Chapter Three
Heidi

I couldn't sleep for the fifth night in a row. So I told Patrick to sleep on my bed and I'd wake him up an hour before he needed to leave for work. Seeing him in my bed was strange. Along with the help of my friends, Matt and Gavin, I painted the entire house in colors that reminded me of my relationship with Andy. I told myself I'd never let another man sleep in my bed. And I thought the meaningful paint in every room would help that, but it didn't. Patrick was right. What we had was different. Special. I can't even explain it, but whatever we had was better than what Andy and I had when our love story was in its cute stage. For a while I lived in denial about the last year of our life together. I erased the bad parts from my heart and chose to remember only the good, but Patrick, warm in my bed, the bed I shared with Andy, made me question all I ever believed about love.

I cooked breakfast. Perfect view of the snow-covered yard while I prepared two plates of French toast and scrambled eggs. Riley babbled in her high chair, banging wooden toys together and sipping my milk from her cup. I smiled at her. She smiled back. Andy's smile. She looked just like her daddy.

I set the plates on the kitchen table, picked up Riley, and went upstairs to wake Patrick. He adjusted to the light, asked the time, and came downstairs with me. I put Riley back in her chair and walked to the front door.

Snow. I loved winter. I opened the door, stepped out in my bare feet, and inhaled.

"Are you crazy?" Patrick said from the kitchen. "Close the door."

I took a deep breath again. The freshness of the white morning made me smile. I love winter like most people love spring. Something about icicles dangling from bare branches makes me feel like living.

A figure caught my eye in the vacant house across the street. I took a step.

"You coming?" Patrick said.

"Yeah." I squinted. The figure backed away from the window.

I went back inside and sat across from Patrick. He took a bite and complimented my cooking. I looked around him to the front windows.

"Everything okay?" he said. "Are you that enamored with the snow?"

"I saw someone in the house over there. Looking at me."

"You're freaking out over nothing. Get those dreams out of your head."

"The house is supposed to be vacant right now. No one lives there."

"It's probably a realtor or something."

"Maybe." I dipped my crunchy French toast in maple syrup and took a bite. "Maybe I am crazy."

"Probably." He smiled.

"Or maybe I'm not." I looked around the room, then whispered, "Andy was in trouble with some people before he died. I can't say anything else, but my fears are legitimate."

Patrick stopped chewing and set his fork down. "Are you kidding me? What is this? A James Bond movie?"

"It's not like that, but it involved a scandal and some money and, I don't know, Andy got really into conspiracy theories the last year of his life and I think his paranoia is rubbing off on me."

"What? You think the man behind the curtain is out to get you?"

"Don't make fun of me." I looked down. "I'm serious."

He touched my hand from across the table. The hand that still wore Andy's ring.

"Sorry." He smiled. "I just have a hard time believing in nightmares. Try to forget about it. There's nothing to worry about."

Easy for him to say. He wasn't alone in a big house with an infant most of the day. My own shadow made me jump nowadays.

We finished breakfast and I left when he did. At his request. He told me to get out of the house and visit some friends. I called Miranda, my friend Matt's sister. She moved to Philly not too long ago and we became close really fast. Maybe because the other girls were married, but also because Lydia was too girly and Ella lived in Lancaster, almost two hours away.

I couldn't spend too much time around her without feeling jealous, so I kept it to a minimum. I know that sounds bad, but I didn't want anymore reasons to be discontent. I needed to be happy for Riley.

Miranda and I met at a small coffee shop in the city. I didn't recognize her at first. Last week her hair was the color of a plum, now bright blue.

"Doesn't that dye ruin your hair?" I said, sitting down across from her.

"Tons of coconut oil and mayonnaise keeps it healthy," she said in her pretend Irish accent. "Well, healthy-ish."

"Why blue?"

"Haven't tried blue yet. Thought I would." She sipped from a steamy mug and nodded to the drink in front of me. "Got your favorite for you."

"Thank you." I warmed my hands with the cup. "How's your brother?"

"Matt? He's good. Work is good. Lydia is good. Baby in the belly is good."

"What about Derek? Are you guys still talking?"

She smiled. "We're friends."

"Friends like you and me? Or friends like Patrick and me?"

"To be determined. I think I'm too much for him. He's so normal."

I laughed. "And we all know you can't handle normal."

"No, but Matt tells me it may be what I need, whether I can handle it or not. What about you? How's Riley's leg? What's it called again?"

"Fibular hemimelia." I smiled at Riley. Such a content and peaceful baby. "I won't have another appointment until it comes time for her first surgery. In the summer."

"What will they do for the first one?"

"Fix her ankle and foot, maybe lengthen a little bit. Then she'll have another surgery when she's almost three. That's when they will start lengthening it more." My eyes glazed over. "I'm really dreading it. I wake up every day wondering why her. What did I do wrong? I just want it to magically heal and be better. I can't imagine putting her through all of this."

"It will be okay. You have a lot of good friends now. What's going on with Patrick?"

"He told me he loves me."

"Wow. About time. And?"

"I never said anything back. I can't." I held up my hand. The ring glis-

21

tened in the sunlight. "I'm still married."

"Man, people think I'm nuts. How long will you spend your life being faithful to a dead man?"

"I said I would forever. I said no man would be worth taking these rings off."

"Patrick isn't worth it?"

I took a drink, ignored her question. She let me ignore it and we filled up the rest of our time with meaningless conversation. Which I needed. Too many serious things in my life. My mind needed a rest.

A text from Patrick popped up on my phone. *You doing okay, butter?*

He called me butter because I put butter on everything. He started calling me buttercup and somehow just went straight to butter.

I texted back. *With Miranda. Talk soon.*

Miranda and I finished up, cleaned our table, and said goodbye. I nursed Riley in the car and put her in her seat. Three minutes after I pulled out of my parking spot she fell asleep.

I drove around, letting her rest and watching her precious face in the mirror. She had no idea that in less than a year she would be getting the first of many surgeries. Her first birthday was coming up. She was already trying to stand and walk. Her right leg didn't touch the ground, but that didn't stop her. Poor thing. Only she didn't see herself as poor. I needed to stop seeing her that way too. Raise her to see it as a gift and not a curse.

I sniffed. Somehow my life took too many bad turns. It all started with that stupid job of Andy's. I told him not to do it. Too much stress. Too much time away from home. He insisted. Looking back I could almost see the life drain out of him.

I stopped at a red light and smiled at Riley. She woke and started playing with the toys hanging from her car seat. I drove to Patrick's chiropractic office and took Riley inside.

We sat in the waiting area. Television playing the latest news from Mwenye's school shooting. A friend of Ella's whose wife claimed he was innocent, but he pleaded guilty and she refused to speak up.

I texted Ella. *How's Tylissa doing?*

She responded fast. *She is okay. Mwenye's arraignment or trial, can't remember … it keeps getting postponed. The media seems to say they are leaning toward death penalty over life in prison. I'm actually at the hospital now. Just parked outside. Visiting Sarah for a few hours with Gavin and James. I'll text you when I'm out. Love ya! :)*

I could relate to Tylissa. I knew the feeling of losing your husband. But Sarah. I couldn't imagine being burned that bad. I would've wanted to die. How horrible to finally get engaged and experience such tragedy before you shared the news with your friends. To lose everything you knew and all that you were. From what Ella told me, Sarah didn't see it that way. She woke up thankful to be alive, whether she still had her gorgeous face or not. And James stood by her, barely leaving her side since their accident. He even wore her engagement ring on a chain around his neck. It would be a while before she could wear it again.

I wanted that kind of love. So bad. I knew I could have it with Patrick if I wanted it, but does love have room for second chances? Does the heart have the ability to give itself fully to two people? I didn't want to divide myself in half. I didn't want to be the second wife. And I didn't want Patrick to be second best either. I almost wished I would've met him before I met Andy, but he's so much older. I would've only been eighteen at the time. He would've been mid-twenties. Might not have worked at that point anyway.

What would it be like to let myself fall in love again? I wondered. Would I have another big wedding? Would I wear a white dress? Could I wear a white dress?

No matter how much I tried, I couldn't imagine. It seemed unnatural. Yet, being with Patrick was the closest thing to natural I'd ever felt.

I sighed, smiled at Riley, and wondered if she would accept Patrick too.

Chapter Four
Patrick

I finished the last client before my lunch break and walked out to the front desk. A familiar beautiful face smiled at me. Make that two familiar beautiful faces.

I lifted Riley and kissed her cheek. She smiled and tried to grab the chain around my neck.

"Didn't expect to see you two lovely ladies here," I said.

Heidi gave me a hug and leaned against the counter. So beautiful in so many ways. Some girls pile on makeup in an effort to try to seem more beautiful than they really are. Not Heidi. She wore light makeup, so light I couldn't see it, but she swore she put a little on. Enough to highlight her features, but not enough to change them. I loved that about her. She always looked bright and natural, even when she seemed sad. Like now.

"How was your time with Miranda?" I said.

"Good," she said. "Just talked to Ella in a text. She said Mwenye is probably going to get the death penalty."

"Doesn't surprise me. That was the worst school shooting our country has ever had."

"But he didn't do it."

"Well, that's what Tylissa says. Maybe it's just a coping mechanism. The guy said himself that he's guilty. Several times."

"Yeah. I don't know. Weird when something like that hits so close to home."

"He had a pretty interesting past. From what I know at least. All that escaping Africa stuff. Maybe he went crazy." Riley reached for Heidi. I handed her over. "Wanna go get lunch?"

She nodded. The weight of life bearing down on her. I could see her

25

strength wilting along with her shoulders. I would've given anything to make her happy, but she wouldn't let me.

We drove to a local pizza shop, ordered a Philly cheesesteak, a large cheese pizza, and an order of fries, then talked sparingly between.

I finally axed the small talk. "You never talk about Andy."

She handed Riley a toy and pretended not to hear me.

"If you want to stay faithful to him then why don't you talk about him?"

"You don't talk about Emily either," she said.

I held up my hand. "I threw my ring out the window last night."

She almost laughed. "What?"

"I'm serious. Look, I'm not going to pretend to be Gavin's grandfather, being faithful to his late wife for decades. I loved Emily. I married her. I wanted to grow old with her and die with her."

"But?"

"But I...." I looked at Riley, then back to Heidi. "I don't know. I would've died for Emily, but she died instead. We never had a normal relationship. I didn't know my wife would die so young. But she did. And my dreams died with her." I took her hand in mine. "This is a new dream. It's like a new life, Heidi. I did love Emily, but my heart died with her and it's almost as though I've been given a new one. I didn't ask for this. It just happened the first time I saw you. I'm alive again and I want nothing more than to be alive next to you."

She inhaled and exhaled. "My dreams never came true, so maybe that's why they won't die with Andy."

"What do you mean?"

"We had a romantic beginning. Doesn't every beginning start off that way? But he started hanging out with his friends more, getting into his job, obsessing over weird things. I kept romance alive by making myself believe what we had was beautiful even when it wasn't. In my own eyes, I had what Gavin and Ella have. In Andy's eyes, I don't know, he just distanced himself from me. I knew he loved me though. It never made sense. Then one day my life changed. He got up for work and I never saw him again. No goodbye. No chance to make it right. Nothing."

"You're saying it feels unresolved?"

"I'm saying I gave my heart to him and never got it back. I'm no longer pretending that what Andy and I had was so amazing that no man could make me want to take this ring off." She made eye contact with me for the first time since we started talking about our ex-spouses. "You are worth it, Patrick. You are more worth it than I ever thought possible." A tear settled in the corner of her eye. "But I don't have a heart to give right now."

I let go of her hand, paid the waiter, and cleaned up the table to make less work for the guy. Riley fussed, obviously bored with the restaurant scene. Heidi took her outside and I came out shortly after.

She sat on a bench, bundled up with Riley. Hat on top of her wind blown hair, she shivered. I helped them to the car and sat in the passengers seat. Emily never let me touch her, and somehow I was okay with that. Initially I was attracted to her, but her problems made me focus more on fixing her than desiring her. I thought I had pretty good self-control, and considering most guys out there, I definitely did, but something about Heidi attracted me to her without my permission. I couldn't look at her without wanting to hold her hand or pull her into me and kiss her until morning. I hated it though. Pure torture.

Everything about her made me question everything I knew about love. I loved Emily. I know I did. But what is love if the heart falls for someone else so fast? Was it real? Did I even know what love was? Why couldn't I stay faithful to Emily like Heidi did to Andy, even in the midst of new love staring her right in the face? Does true love stay faithful even after death?

Question upon question. No answers. More than anything, I guess what I feared was if the heart was capable of loving twice and, if so, is it possible for someone to marry the wrong person?

Chapter Five
Heidi

Patrick and I decided to stop talking about whatever relationship existed between us and live without asking so many questions. Weeks passed as we ignored the growing passion between us. I hid my feelings well, or so I thought, but not well enough. He knew how I felt and that killed me. I couldn't choose between Andy and Patrick. I almost wished someone could choose for me. I'd wake up two years from now and the decision would be made.

I washed the dishes as Riley played on a blanket by my feet. Andy's mom kept leaving messages on my phone asking about her surgery, but I couldn't bring myself to respond. She never asked about me, only Riley. And my daughter's leg wasn't about to become a topic for the gossip train to pass along.

After washing the last dish, I took Riley to the living room, set her down with some wooden blocks, and checked the mailbox. Another cold day. Freezing, really. I grabbed the mail and noticed a figure in the house across the street again. It moved from the window, like the last time.

I closed the door, locked it, and grabbed my phone from the couch. Just as I started to text Patrick I saw a realtor walk out with an older couple. Really losing my mind, I thought.

I sat on the floor with Riley, thinking about my past and considering my future. Earlier in the morning I had looked up the word "love" in the dictionary app on my phone, but I wasn't satisfied with the results. Defined as either a deep affection or sex. Everything I found reduced love to a feeling. That's it. A simple feeling or emotion. Nothing more.

I thought of Gavin's wedding speech. How he described love as Ella, his bride, and life. He said the two went hand-in-hand. It sounded nice.

She cried. He cried. His dying grandfather listened from a cot set up beside them. It was romantic and I was happy for them, but it still didn't make sense to me. This thing called love. Well, it did make sense, but it stopped making sense the day Patrick walked into my life and tempted me to walk away from the life I lived for so long. The life that made sense. At least to me.

Oh, if only Andy could tell me that it's okay to move on, I thought, then looked at Riley. She smiled and crawled toward me. So much of Andy lived and breathed inside of that little girl. And outside too. Could I really take my rings off?

Too many "what if's." Too many disconnected lines. How could love make sense to me? Nothing did anymore. Nothing.

I called Ella.

"Hey, Heidi," she said, sounding a little too happy.

"I'm so sorry I haven't returned your call. It's been a little crazy."

"Is everything okay?"

"As okay as it can be, I guess."

"Gavin and I are going to be in Philly tomorrow. We were wondering if you wanted to get together with us and Matt and Lydia. We will be at Matt's house. I think Miranda and Patrick will be there, too."

I didn't want to, but knowing Patrick would be there, I felt a magnetic draw.

After he told me he loved me and I didn't say it back, he became distant. Didn't reach for my hand or come over as much. I missed him. So I told her I'd be there and texted Patrick to see if we could drive together. Of course he said yes, though I worried if another girl stole his heart. Someone older. More willing to love him back. I wanted to scream to him that I loved him, but I couldn't. Not yet. Not until my heart no longer chased the man I married, for better or worse.

ELLA NEVER SAID SO, BUT I COULD TELL SHE DIDN'T APPROVE of me falling in love again, so I thought I'd pull her aside at Matt's house and ask her some honest questions. I didn't think it would be so difficult, but her hand was practically stitched to Gavin's hand and it would take surgery to pry them apart. They were always madly in love with each other, but since the wedding they became more touchy in public. I envied her beauty and charm. And her movie-like love story. Some people have all the luck, I guess.

I played with Riley on the floor by Patrick's feet. She loved being on the floor so she could reach for toys and crawl around. Avoiding my thoughts, I tuned back into the conversation.

"So, we have news," Lydia said as she pulled Matt's arm closer to her.

"You're having twins?" Gavin said, laughing.

"Funny that you joke about that," Matt said.

"You're kidding." Ella jumped up and hugged them both.

"Slow down woman," Matt said. "I was kidding. We just wanted to tell everyone that yesterday we had our first ultrasound and it's a healthy little boy."

Everyone congratulated them. I couldn't help but linger on the word "healthy." When I had my first ultrasound for Riley it took two hours, but I never had a baby so I didn't know that was abnormal. The nurse wasn't very nice. She kept saying she couldn't get a good shot of Riley's leg and her face grew red with frustration. I couldn't wait to leave, but they made me stay.

My midwife came back in the room to talk to me. "You are having a baby girl," she said. "But there's a problem with one of her legs. It's hard to tell right now, but one of her legs appears to be shorter than the other and somewhat malformed. We will follow up at a different place. They do more in-depth ultrasounds. We can talk more once we get to that point." She hugged me, but I didn't cry. Not until a few weeks later when a doctor gave me the option of abortion.

I wanted to be happy for Lydia and her healthy baby boy, but I kept thinking, why me, why Riley, why couldn't my baby be healthy too?

Patrick tapped my shoulder. I jumped.

"You okay?" he said, offering me a hand to stand up.

"I'm okay." And okay was about it. Good, wonderful, amazing, undeniably happy—that wasn't me. Okay. I could agree with "okay."

I hugged Lydia and Matt, congratulated them, and saw Ella alone on the couch. Gavin nowhere in sight. Miracle of all miracles. So I sat down beside her and got right to the point.

"Do you think I should stay faithful to Andy?" I said.

Ella leaned back, smiled. "Where'd that come from?"

"I need to know what you think. You and Gavin have something rare. I'm not expecting to ever compete with what you guys have, but since you are the romance guru I thought I'd ask your opinion."

Gavin stepped back into the room. Ella nodded to him and he walked over to Matt. They spoke without talking. I loved that.

"Well, the person I was before I met Gavin would have told you to never take your rings off and to love Andy as though he were still alive."

"But the new Ella wouldn't?"

"The new Ella has been changed by Sarah's experience and marriage."

"How so?"

"I've watched my best friend go through torment. First she had cancer. A few months after her remission James proposed and they had the fire accident. I've seen her smile throughout this incredible pain, and I've seen James stand by her constantly. You can't visit Sarah without seeing him. He's there. By her side every day."

"What about Abby?"

"She stays with his parents. He is coming home this weekend actually. Sarah insisted that he come back for Abby."

"Okay, so this has changed you and now what would you say to me?"

She made eye contact with Gavin. "I'd say not every love story is written the same, and you have to follow your heart where it takes you."

"Do you believe in soul-mates?"

"Yes." She didn't hesitate.

"Do you believe you can marry the wrong person?"

She looked down. Thought about it.

"Do you believe you can have two soul-mates?"

She took a deep breath and held my arm. "Hollywood tends to emotionalize love. The movies make it all about attraction and feelings. That's why I used to feel the way I did. I was shaped by our culture. Movies. Music. All of it. Since then I've seen real love. And Gavin's made it a point to show me that love is more than that. It's deeper. And it's different for every person. I've seen Tylissa stick by her husband even when he is seen as a terrible monster by the world around her. I've seen James stick by

Sarah, even though she went from being one of the most beautiful girls I've ever known, to someone who will now spend her life turning heads away because of her scars. So what I'm saying to you is that you are the only person who can answer these questions for yourself. All I know is that when your soul becomes so entwined with another soul that you can't breathe when he's gone, you have become soul-mates. When you can't live without him and he feels the exact same way. Can that happen twice? You tell me."

I watched Patrick as Riley wrapped her arms around his neck and squeezed. He stopped talking to the guys to pay attention to her, to love my little girl, then he went back to their conversation. Honestly, I didn't know if I felt that way about Patrick. We were never together, so how could I know how I'd feel if he were gone?

Ella interrupted my thoughts. "When your head hits the pillow at night, who do you think about?"

"Hate to sound so unromantic, but I think moreso about the mess I am in than I do a single person."

"Well, think about it." She stood. "And when you know, you know."

I walked to Patrick, felt his arm brush against mine as I reached for Riley. He smiled. I tried to.

I spent the rest of the night listening and watching the couples around me. As hard as it was for me to admit, I think I missed Andy more than I wanted Patrick. Yes, Patrick was more attractive. Yes, he was sweeter and more sensitive. Yes, he loved me more than Andy ever seemed to.

Yes, yes, yes.

But Andy had one thing that Patrick didn't have.

The leftover fragments of what used to be my heart.

Chapter Six
Patrick

After talking with Ella, Heidi told me she wanted to take a break from seeing each other for a while. I didn't understand, but told her I'd do whatever she needed. As soon as I got home I called Ella to find out what she said to Heidi.

"Nothing bad," she said. Cars passed in the background. "She might be taking a break to see how much she misses you when you're gone. Just plan something romantic and surprise her with it when she is ready to see you again."

"First of all," I said. "I have no idea how to plan something romantic. Second of all, what if she misses Andy more? I don't want to hurt her. I need to step back and just be her friend. I think that's what she needs the most."

"You'd be a better judge of that than me."

"Pretty amazed that you're even supportive of this. Thought you wanted her to stay faithful to Andy forever?"

"I did. Things change," she said. "Gavin and I wouldn't remarry, but every love story is different."

I hung up with her, took a shower, and got ready for bed. A picture of Emily caught my eye. The little card from her funeral. I held it in my hands, touched her face. I remember the one time she allowed me to kiss her on the lips. Our wedding day. People always asked me why I married someone who wouldn't let me kiss her. The answer is simple. She needed somewhere to live and medical insurance for her medication. I was her house and medical insurance. She was my life. I thought for sure if I helped her she'd love me back. And she did, don't get me wrong. She did in her own way. Just not the way most wives love their husbands.

I imagined Heidi's face. Sweet smile, pink cheeks, captivating golden eyes. I loved the way her nose crinkled when she laughed. And the right dimple that appeared when she smiled. Man, she was the picture of beauty.

I picked up my phone to text her. I typed *I love you*, but deleted it and turned the phone off.

I told her I'd fight for her and be there for her until my last breath, but how could I? She loved Andy. She didn't love me.

I admired that. I really did. Never knew someone more faithful.

Maybe I needed to let go. Move on. Find a girl who wanted me as much as I wanted her.

Story of my freaking life.

AS A CHIROPRACTIC DOCTOR A LOT OF WOMEN CAME INTO MY office. Beautiful women with cute personalities. Never noticed as much until Heidi stopped talking to me. Of course I always ignored the subtle flirtations. I'm a doctor and don't want to get sued for sexual harassment. So I'm careful when I work and very serious.

But I'm not going to lie, when I walked out to the waiting room and called for Myra my heart stopped. Then I realized I met her before. She was the Filipino girl at Gavin's old house in Philly. A friend of a friend. Referred to me by Lydia.

Gorgeous. I hadn't noticed before. My eyes were only on Heidi. Now they were opened. I didn't flirt with her, but she caught my attention for sure. As I helped her out I didn't say a word beyond the normal professional words I always say. When I finished she stood and put her hands on her hips.

"I think I feel a little better," she said through pink lips. "Thank you."

"No problem," I said.

"How's everything with Heidi?"

"Not sure. She is taking a break from talking to me."

"Oh, I'm sorry to hear that."

I shrugged. "I want the best for her. Whatever that is."

She stood there. Looking up at me. Analyzing my face as I blushed.

"When you find the one for you, you'll know," she said.

"Why does everyone say that? Like love is some kind of riddle to be figured out. I'm not so sure about that. I've been married before and my wife died. Now this. I think I go after people who are a challenge." I put my hands in my pockets. "No idea why. I don't even know if I know what love is anymore."

"Sure you do."

"No. I really have no idea. All this mumbo jumbo talk of soul-mates and one person being the only person for you. What's that mean for people like me? Doomed to be single for life since I already married someone and she's gone?"

"I believe that most people only have one soul-mate, but some of us need more than one. So our hearts are broken and when they are put back together they are something new. A new heart for a new soul-mate."

"What about you?"

She blushed. "What about me?"

"Have you found your soul-mate?"

"I think so, but it's hard because I have to go back to the Philippines before I overstay my visa for school. I don't know what we're going to do." She exhaled. "Do you remember Reese from Gavin's party last year?"

"I do. Nice guy."

"Very nice."

"Lucky too."

She smiled. "Follow your heart, but bring your mind. You will find your answers."

We said our goodbyes. Everyone seemed to know everything about love. Everyone but Heidi and me. Honestly, I thought everyone was tainted by Hollywood and Disney. Ella said it herself once. Except Ella had no room to talk. Her and Gavin had something better than the movies.

Ugh, I'm not one to complain, but can a guy get a break?

All I wanted was someone to share my life with. Heidi seemed so perfect. We fit together in ways we needed, not just ways we wanted. We were right for each other. How do you let go of someone when their heart is set on someone else?

Chapter Seven
Heidi

I spent most days inside after I told Patrick I needed some space. Thankfully I worked mostly from home as an interior designer, so I didn't need to go out if I didn't want to. Unless I needed to go to a clients house or buy some things for their project, or for myself. Like food, which I now needed.

I found a forum online for moms who delayed solid foods with their babies until after a year. With all of Riley's soon-to-be surgeries I figured I would do anything I could to make her healthier. Coming up on her first birthday, I decided to let her try a few things, but needed a quick market visit first.

A well-tinted vehicle pulled away from the house as I got into my car. I'm normally not a paranoid person, but since Andy uncovered that scandal at work I really did fear for my life. I hated that he discovered the truth in that mess, and I know it was good of him to insist on telling the truth and testifying in court, but I didn't want him to. I didn't want him to do half the things he did when we first got married. He said he needed to provide, to be a good husband. So I let him, wondering why he thought being a good husband meant making money. All I wanted was a hug and a kiss goodnight before bed, but that was too much to ask. He was always too tired, too burned out, too paranoid. I guess he had a good reason to be.

Never in a million years did I think I'd have gang members after my husband. Or me. I swear it seemed like someone was still following me. I remember all the threats when Andy first offered to testify in court. One night we were lying in bed and Andy woke me up screaming, begging me to get in the car with him and hide. Confused, I followed him. We drove away and parked behind the grocery store, fearing shadows and passing cars, until daylight settled on the car.

I still had nightmares. I don't know. I didn't mind dying, but I had a baby now. And yes, I didn't want anything to happen to her. Maybe it was all in my head.

In my head or not, I wanted to call Patrick, but I refused. Really needed to wait and see if I missed him. Test out the waters and see if I loved him or if that was all in my head too.

I grabbed some produce from a local farmer's market and some milk and eggs, then headed back home with Riley. She never made a peep. Such a sweetie.

I took her inside the house, then came back to get the food. After I got everything put away I took Riley upstairs to give her a bath and noticed a pair of Patrick's pants on my bed. I didn't remember getting them out and panicked again.

So I texted Miranda. *Hey, can you come over? I have a strange feeling someone is stalking me.*

Are you serious? she messaged back.

Yeah. You busy?

Be there in fifteen.

I undressed Riley and sat her in the tub. A door closed downstairs. Quietly. But I still heard it. I picked Riley up, locked the bathroom door, put her back in the bath, and tried to calm my heart rate. Pretty sure my heart wanted to climb out of my chest and into my throat, but got stuck and decided to throb in my ears.

I hated being a single mother. Hated it. People thought I handled myself so well. And maybe I did, but not at night. Alone. In a dark house with creaky sounds. Patrick tried to convince me that I was imagining sounds. I don't know. Maybe.

Miranda called when she arrived and I met her at the door.

"Are you okay?" she said.

"I don't know. Why don't you move in with me until you figure out what you're doing?"

She made herself at home on the couch and pulled a book out of her purse. "We'll talk when you get Riley to sleep."

"Moved on to turquoise hair now?"

"Yeah. Kind of matches the weather. Like icicles."

I shook my head and brought Riley to her bedroom. We had a simple bedtime routine. A short book, she nursed, then I put her in her crib and she blinked herself to sleep. No pacifier needed. I am so glad I never had to let her cry-it-out because I don't know if I could've done it.

I kissed her goodnight and went back downstairs. Miranda put her book down and turned toward me.

"What's that look for?" I said.

"Come on," she said. "You know you love him. Why can't you admit it?"

"Do I love him? Or do I love the idea of him? The idea of having a man in my heart again?"

"You tell me."

"Everything is too confusing. I had to choose between amputating my daughters leg and giving her less surgeries throughout her life, or lengthening it and having her suffer for years to keep her leg. That's hard. And if that's not enough, now I find myself torn between the memory of Andy that still lives in my heart and the hope of Patrick that wants to live in my heart. I can't choose this time. Someone needs to decide for me."

"You mean you want an airplane to write your answers in the sky?"

"Yes. That would work."

We laughed.

"Did I tell you I'm considering moving to Boston?" she said, flipping her turquoise hair behind her shoulder.

"Do you ever stay still?"

"I can't. Not who I am."

"What about Ella's brother? I thought you liked him?"

"Kinda. We talk a lot, but he's so unbelievably boring. He's so settled. I mean, the guy wear's the same color every time I see him."

"And that's a bad thing? Maybe you need some stability."

"Maybe. Doubt it though. I need adventure. Life is meant to be lived."

"And you think people like Derek don't live?"

"Precisely."

I thought about her words for so long that she picked her book back up and read until she fell asleep. I turned the light off and went to my room. I wasn't content in my singleness. Not at all. I didn't want a friend. I wanted a husband. Someone to experience life with. All of life. Ups and downs and in-betweens.

MIRANDA LEFT EARLY SATURDAY MORNING. SHE WORKED AT a tattoo studio owned by Dee, Ella's friend. She didn't do the tattoos though. Funny. Weird hair and crazy clothes, but anti-tattoos. She ran the desk and cleaned up. Couldn't find a use for her psychology degree and she grew to hate the entire field anyway. So tattoo shop it was. Dee did all the tattoos along with her friend, Griffin. Actually was a nice place if you're into that kinda thing. Reminded me of something out of a slightly romantic Tim Burton movie, if you can imagine such a place.

I worked a little while Riley napped. Had a client who wanted to redo her basement. Not the most thrilling job in the world, but I needed to pay the bills and felt bad that Patrick gave so much of his money to help me stay on my feet.

Something clicked downstairs. The front door creaked. Heart racing, I crept down the hallway and peered down the steps. A shadow moved. I put my hand on my chest and reached for my phone. The figure moved toward the bottom of the steps. I screamed so loud Riley immediately woke.

"It's me," Patrick said. "I couldn't handle being apart."

"Let me calm Riley down. Wait downstairs."

I nursed Riley and rocked her back to sleep, heart still beating a million miles a minute, but she woke back up so I took her downstairs. Patrick waited on the couch. Tired eyes and disheveled hair. Obviously sleep deprived. I set Riley on the floor with some blocks and stuffed animals, then sat next to Patrick. He breathed in as though it were painful to do so, then looked at me, waiting for me to say something, anything. I hid my eyes behind my hands and rubbed my face. The air between us, warmed with anticipation, yet cooled by my unwillingness, waited to be filled with words I couldn't give.

Shaking, I tried to pull the rings off my finger. They barely moved. I twisted and tugged harder. Nothing. Pat looked away and shook his head. Maybe it was a sign? I went to the kitchen, poured dish soap on my finger and yanked on the rings.

Nothing.

Absolutely nothing.

Pat stood behind me. I wanted to take his arms and wrap them around my body. *Kiss me*, I pleaded inside. *Just do it. Do something. Make me feel like this will work out. Give me a little hope.*

I turned and faced him. He bit his lip and looked at the ring I couldn't get off. His eyes said, "It's okay." But his lips stayed far from mine. I watched them move, looking for words to say, but saying nothing. We stared at each other. Riley banged toys in the background. I couldn't take it anymore.

I pressed my lips against his and held them there, waiting for him to kiss me back, for him to take over my heart and never let go.

He pulled away and put his finger over my lips. "This isn't how you want it to go."

"I'm sick of following my mind, Pat. I want to follow my heart for once." I moved toward him. "Let me."

"Emotions aren't always from the heart."

"I don't understand."

"I'm sorry I came back. You need more time. It's not right. When the ring comes off, call me. Until then, know that I'm waiting for you."

"But I want you now." A tear fell to the floor between us. "Don't go."

He shook his head, held back his own tears, and walked to the living room. Riley reached up for him and he squeezed her, kissed her cheek, and set her back down. I stood by the dining room table, heart on the floor next to my tear-soaked dreams. He rubbed his face, then looked at the ceiling. I didn't understand.

"I will always love you," he said. "Always. Take more time like you wanted. We'll know when it's right."

I let him walk out the door. Confused, broken, I stood in the same place until Riley ached for me to hold her. I was so tired of being needed. I loved Riley. I loved her so much and I was happy to be her mother, but I wanted to need someone. And I did. I needed a husband, a best friend, a partner in all things life threw my way. I finally knew I needed him and he told me to keep thinking about it. *I know I need you*, I wanted to scream to him as he drove away. I yanked at the ring on my finger again, hoping it would slip off and I could run after Pat, begging him to come back, to come into my heart and never leave, but it wouldn't budge.

I tried over and over, used the entire bottle of dish soap, and still . . . my past wanted to stay my present.

Chapter Eight
Patrick

I missed her. No getting around it. The girl stole my heart without me realizing it, but I respected her and wanted to give her space. So I did. Even though I almost blew it. Seeing her try to rip those rings off her finger killed me. She wanted to be with me. I could tell. Maybe even needed to. But I wanted more than that. I wanted it to be right, to be natural. Not forced. I needed to give her more time or she would end up regretting it in the future. But I also listened to Ella's advice and decided to plan something romantic.

Ella told me to make a scrapbook of our memories so far and our dreams for the future. Gavin offered to draw some pictures for it. So I decided to visit them in Lancaster and work on it with them.

I parked in front of their house and sighed. They were the kind of couple I needed to prepare myself to be around. They could either inspire you or make you feel horrible about yourself, depending on how you felt that day. They were almost too good together. In their physical appearance and personality. Most people who didn't know them well thought they faked their love for each other. It's that amazing. Too good to be true.

I walked up to the door and knocked. Gorgeous house. Used to be Gavin's grandfathers house. Built before 1900 and incredible.

Ella answered the door with a smile, as always. "Ah, look who it is."

"Yeah." I hugged her. "Where's the man of the house?"

"He's outside tending to the winter veggies."

"Winter veggies?"

"Yeah. We decided to use some of this land to plant our own vegetables and we found some things that grow even through the winter." She led me to the kitchen. "Want some soup? Just made some baked potato soup, all local dairy products."

I laughed. "Surprised you guys don't have your own cows yet." I looked around the kitchen. White cabinets. White table. White everywhere. "Love what you guys did with the kitchen, but don't you plan to have kids?"

She smiled. "We do. Isn't this so refreshing though?"

"It is. But it may not be once you have a toddler."

She shrugged. "No word from Heidi?"

I shook my head. "You?"

"She hasn't returned my texts in days."

Gavin walked in the door and smiled. "Hey, man. How's it been?"

I hugged him. "Been okay, I guess. With Christmas coming up I was thinking of giving this to Heidi as a gift on Christmas Eve."

"Good idea." He washed his hands and took his hat off.

Ella wrapped her arms around him. "I missed you."

"You too, love," he said.

"You missed each other when you were less than a football field apart?" I laughed. "Can't believe you guys aren't pregnant yet."

"Actually," Ella said.

"Are you serious?"

"We haven't told anyone yet. We were going to think of a creative way to tell everyone," Gavin said.

Ella kissed his cheek. "We think it's a honeymoon baby."

"When's the due date?" I asked.

"Early August," she said. "There's a natural birthing place thirty minutes from here that we will be going to. I'm so excited. We find out if it's a boy or girl in March."

"Any names?"

"We aren't sure yet. We like Gwendolyn and Adelaine for a girl, and Emerson and Dylan for a boy."

I laughed. "Gwendolyn would be pretty, but Gavin and Gwen is like Gavin Rossdale and Gwen Stefani."

Gavin laughed. "Didn't think of that. Guess it would be Adelaine then."

"Enough about us," Ella said. "Let's get started on this scrapbook.

I bought all the supplies for it."

"You are too much."

Chapter Nine
Heidi

Patrick didn't text me. No calls, no texts, no emails. Every day I wanted to text him and tell him I loved him, but I couldn't get the rings off. I tried everything and I couldn't muster the nerve to break them. Everything about it felt wrong. I guess I understood what Pat meant. It needed to be right. But how could it be? How can you fall in love again in a situation like this? Maybe the person is meant to be your best friend simply because you can't survive life alone. Maybe it's not meant to be some amazing love story for the masses.

I set my orange juice on the kitchen counter and saw a figure run by the window. I stood on my tip-toes, but couldn't see anything. A rush of heat went from my head to my feet. Someone was out there. I listened to make sure Riley was still asleep, then looked through every window of the house. Didn't see anything. I locked the basement door, sat on the couch, and heard a tapping sound in the kitchen. A dark figure stood at the back door. All in black. I didn't scream this time. Didn't really care if I died. So I sat there and watched. He tried to open the door, looked around as though someone were after him, then took off his mask.

Photographs of the past piled up in my mind. Stained memories of what could have been. He moved his arms frantically, motioning for me to open the door. I did.

He stood in front of me, out of breath. A day I dreamed about for so long felt more like a nightmare. My heart, as if it could endure more damage, willingly followed him to the bedroom.

I sat on the bed. "What are you doing here?"

"I told you I'd come back if they stopped chasing me."

"But Andy, you made me promise. I told everyone you died. I told them you wanted to be cremated, just like you said. Even have this stupid thing of fake ashes in our living room. I've lived this lie for a year now. You told me you wouldn't come back. You said for me to move on and live. You made me promise."

My body shook. I'm not sure if I wanted him to hold me or not. He didn't. I curled up on the bed and heard Riley cry.

"Is that her?" he said.

I nodded. "I named her Riley, just like you wanted."

He smiled. "Can I see her?"

"Andy, this isn't fair. What am I supposed to tell everyone? They will think we are both insane."

"Look, I have a plan. I want to take you and Riley to Germany. I know someone there. We can start a new life."

"Germany?" I wiped my face. "I can't go to Germany. Riley has something called fibular hemimelia. She needs a lot of care from some good doctors down in Baltimore. I need to live close to make sure she gets the care she needs."

"What's fibular hemimelia?"

"I can't believe you're back."

"You don't seem happy about it."

"I don't know what to feel. You've been gone. I've pretended you were dead and started to believe it myself. I met new friends. Started a life without you. I've been a single mom. A widow. And all this time couldn't tell a soul that you were really just hiding. Who knows where. Did you sleep with another woman?"

He touched my left hand, ran his fingers over the rings he gave me when he promised a beautiful life of love and laughter, then pointed to his left hand. "I've kept my ring on too. And I've kept my promises."

"Where have you been living?"

"In the woods."

"You're kidding," I laughed, realizing Riley calmed down for the first time without me.

"I am. I don't want to say in case they are listening."

"Andy, I can't live like this. You've created this world of fear and suspicion and it drove me nuts before you left. I don't want to raise Riley like this. It's too much."

He looked around the room. "You've done a good job decorating the house."

I nodded.

He touched my neck and pulled my face toward his. Inches from my lips, he whispered, "I love you. Runaway with me so we can be together."

I moved back. Away from the lips that wanted to kiss me. Away from my husband. My husband. The one who told me to think of him as dead for the rest of my life. His shoulders dropped. His eyes too. Everything downcast. Including our marriage. I exhaled and shoved my face into a pillow.

"Heidi," he said. "You realize I did this for you? I didn't want you to get hurt."

I tossed the pillow aside and slammed my hand on the bed. "This is torture. Don't you understand? Mafias and money and banks and scandals. How do you expect me to live in some kind of action movie? I want a peaceful life. I don't want to live in another country. Why did you have to testify against these people? You should've left it alone."

"Please, Heidi. Come with me. I can't stay here. I'm on so many black-lists it's not funny."

"None of this is funny."

He sighed. "Do you still love me?"

I leaned back and slipped under the sheets. Without making a sound I gripped the blanket, pulled it over my head, and wept and screamed in silence. Andy touched my leg. Why me? Why me? I thought over and over. And the one image that I couldn't erase from my closed eyelids was Patrick's face, smiling at me from across the table. Eyes intent on loving me. In a way the man sitting on my bed, my first love and husband, never did. Because he never could.

CLOCK SAID 5:57 A.M. I ROLLED OVER AND SAW ANDY'S FACE. HE fell asleep there hours and hours ago, as though he hadn't slept in years. I played with Riley, put her to sleep, then fell asleep beside him with a severe ache in my chest. I looked at the clock again. A new day. A new day so different than everything I hoped for the day before. I watched him sleep and replayed our memories. So many sweet memories early on, but they were dampened by the most recent ones. He changed. We all change. I know I did too. But some of us risk everything and climb up the mountain while others spend their lives digging their graves. Andy stopped living long ago. He truly died when I was forced to pretend that he did, but his heart was still beating beside me. His lungs still sucked in air and blew it back out. But I feared the darkness that enveloped him. Riley had enough to worry about. She didn't need this.

He opened his eyes and turned up the corner of his mouth in a half smile.

But . . . it didn't matter what I wanted. Hasn't mattered in a long time. Andy was my husband. A wife is to be faithful to her husband. I needed to erase my dreams of Patrick and keep my heart where it had been all along. In my husbands hands.

"This isn't easy," I said.

"It's like I've come back from the dead." He laughed.

If only that were true, I thought.

"Look, there's gotta be some way for Riley to get help in another country. Let's look into it."

"Maybe, but these guys specialize in it. People travel from all over the world to come here."

"I never thought I'd be able to come home." He rolled to his back. "I thought you'd be happy."

"I'm a widow. Everyone I know thinks I'm a widow. To be with you I have to leave everything I know and go somewhere new. What if you leave again and I'm forced to do the same thing there? I can't play these games, Andy. This is my life."

"Do you love me, Heidi?" He took my hand. Gone were the days of excitement and butterflies.

"You're my husband. Of course I love you."

"That's not what I'm asking. Are you still in love with me?"

"I don't know who you are. How can I be?"

He exhaled. "I'm still me. Look, yes or no. Do you love me?"

I looked away, then back to his eyes.

"Then why does everyone else matter? You can make friends wherever we go."

"Real friends? I can just imagine you asking me to change my name and pretend to be someone else. For the first time in my life I feel like I'm getting somewhere. My job is good. Riley has great doctors. I have found friends, true friends, who I admire and want to be around. I like it here. I don't want to uproot everything because of some unjustified fears you have."

Riley made sounds from her room. I stood and went to her, then brought her back to my bed, our bed. Andy sat up and smiled.

"Hey, Riley," he said. "It's your daddy."

She smiled and reached for his nose.

"Wow," he said. "I didn't think she would be so comfortable with me so fast."

"She loves people."

"She is so pretty. Look at those dark eyes and hair." A tear made its way to his lips. And another. He sniffed. "I never thought I'd get to meet her."

I wiped his tears with the back of my hand. He cupped my hand in his and took a deep breath, then tried to speak, but his lips only quivered in silence.

"I can't believe you kept your rings on." He let more tears fall. "I'm so sorry, Heidi. I'm sorry for ruining your life."

I looked at Riley. "You didn't ruin my life. Look at this little girl. She's so much like you and she means so much to me."

"But I don't mean much to you anymore?"

"Andy, what do you want me to say? I'm sorry, but you've been dead to me for the last year and as far as I knew you were never coming back. It drove me crazy. I've battled back and forth between moving on or waiting around for you, just in case. All because you had to snitch on some people who like to shoot guns. This is so ridiculous. I'm willing to be with you, but it needs to be here. I'm not moving anywhere. I don't care if they kill me."

He shook his head and flopped back onto the pillows. "I like the colors you chose for this room. What made you pick them?"

"Funny you ask. I painted every room in the house to resemble a part of our relationship. I thought it would help me keep you alive and keep myself sane. This room resembles our wedding night and also your fake death that I told everyone was true. It became real to me though. I had to believe you died."

"What are the colors?"

"Crushed berry and charcoal, I think."

"It's nice. How does it symbolize my fake death?"

"Blood on asphalt."

"Do you think I'm crazy?"

"A little, yes."

He stood and pulled his jeans over his hips. Had been a while since I saw a man barely dressed. I looked away. Riley wanted to nurse, so I took her back to her room and fed her. So strange to have Andy back. For so long I dreamed of this day. I thought it would've been different. Like a mother and child waiting at the airport for their soldier to come home. Instead it felt like the sad ending to the story just got sadder. Maybe I would've been happier if it weren't for Patrick. Maybe I needed to move away and start over.

I cuddled Riley and sighed. Most women would love to bring their husbands back from the dead. Me? I wasn't sure. Life with Andy wouldn't be stable.

He came into the nursery and smiled as though life were perfectly normal. I found some strange resemblance of courage and smiled. He knelt down beside me, touched my foot.

"Sweetheart," he said. "I will do whatever you want. I just want to be with you. Tell me what you want."

My eyes glazed over and his face blurred. One tear. Two. Three. I didn't know what I wanted. I loved him. I loved what we had before this mess. Everything changed. Everything confused me. I didn't know. And why, every time I closed my eyes, did Patrick grace the backs of my eyelids? I was a married woman. I should've never let my heart open up to Patrick.

"Let me think about it," I said. "Maybe we can move somewhere. I need some time to think through everything."

He kissed my cheek and slid his hand across Riley's face. I had a daughter now. Another life to consider. What would be best for her?

"Why do you love me?" I said.

"I can't answer that. Too many reasons. I love everything about you. Always have."

"Give me five reasons."

He thought about it. "You aren't playing the romantic game again are you?"

"What romantic game?"

"Where you hunt for something romantic?"

"No. Was just wondering."

To be honest, I was done with hunting.

Chapter Ten
Patrick

I woke up on Christmas Eve to snowflakes on my window and sweat all over my body. You could say I was nervous. Or you could say I was freaked out beyond belief. Both were true.

What if she didn't choose me? She hadn't tried to contact me since I left. Or anyone else for that matter. I wasn't a heart on the sleeve kind of guy. I kept it tucked inside my shirt and put it on my sleeve only when I fell in love. Which so far had only been twice. Rejected the first time, I didn't want to be rejected again. But Heidi was worth the risk.

I showered and put on my best shirt, a nice pair of dark jeans, and the only pair of nice boots I owned. Then I stared in the mirror for five minutes having pretend conversations with Heidi where I professed my love, she finally told me she loved me, and we embraced and kissed for the first time. The first real time. I put my hands in my pockets and said goodbye to my reflection.

The drive to Heidi's was longer than normal because of the snow. I took my time and considered all of the possible outcomes. If she flat out rejected me, I'd move on. If she cried and hugged me, but couldn't answer right away, I'd give her more time. And finally, if she told me she loved me I'd buy an engagement ring the next day. Out of curiosity, I'd been looking at rings for weeks. I knew exactly what she would like and it looked nothing like the solitaire diamond Andy gave her. Not that I felt the need to compete with him. I wanted her to love him and retain his memory in her heart forever. He was Riley's father. I knew she'd end up calling me daddy eventually, at least I imagined so. But she shouldn't forget who her real dad was either. That was important to me. I knew my place in Heidi's heart and the thought of Andy didn't threaten me. More than anything I felt threatened by my own feelings. I didn't want to ruin things by pushing too much, but I literally ached when I couldn't see her. Yes, I loved Emily a lot and went through quite a bit of pain when she died, but I never longed for her with the same intensity I longed for Heidi. Maybe it was my age. A few years older. A few experiences wiser. Life taught me a lot the last few years and I didn't have energy for games. My heart wanted to be with this woman and I couldn't change that. Believe me, I tried. Seeing that ring on her finger made it easy to want to move on, but every time I tried I only realized how much more I loved her. How much I'd give up anything for her happiness.

I pulled up in front of her house and wiped my palms on my jeans. Lights were on in her living room and Riley's room. I turned the car off and waited until I could see my breath in the air.

Her gift, neatly wrapped in pink and silver stripes, sat next to me. The gift that spoke of our relationship. The gift that would hopefully show her that what we had was unique. That our future together would be amazing.

I tucked the present under my arm, opened my door, and set off to the unknown.

My hands shook as I knocked on the door. No answer. I peeked through the curtains. Nothing but the glowing Christmas tree and mountain of presents underneath. I knocked again and waited.

Still nothing.

I fumbled around my pockets and pulled out my keys. Still had her spare. I unlocked the door and entered. Quiet. Didn't want to wake anyone. The pine scent of the tree filled the air. Along with some kind of baked cinnamon treat. Maybe an apple pie. I walked toward the tree to set the gift with the others and heard a sound.

I stopped and listened. A slight creaking, rocking sound. Probably Heidi putting Riley to sleep. I sat on the couch, wondering if I should wait for her to come downstairs or just leave the gift. The note at the end told her what to do next. I liked the idea of not being there when she opened it. I stood and the rocking sound increased. I walked to the bottom of the steps. A man grunted, obviously in pleasure, then the rocking slowed and stopped.

Didn't take much to realize the woman I desired with all my heart refused to be with me, but was sleeping with another man. On Christmas

Eve of all nights.

I took the gift back to my car and sped off, slipping on the ice and re-gaining control of my car. Why did I fall in love with women who couldn't love me back? I wanted to punch myself in the face. Over and over until blood poured from my nose and spelled out the words, *It's never worth it.*

Chapter Eleven
Heidi

Okay, so he was my husband. It's not like I could deny him my body. In his eyes, I had no reason to. His return from the "dead" should've elated me, but for the life of me I couldn't get Patrick out of my head. Andy practically forced himself on me, thinking it was romantic, you know, with the snow dancing outside on Christmas Eve. So I laid there as he used my body for pleasure. No, not just physically. He needed to feel connected to me again. To feel like we were still one, even though the time and distance had torn us apart.

I let him do his thing as I imagined Patrick. An adulteress. That's what I felt like. It killed me. Faithfulness was important to me. Being a good wife, mother, friend. Those things were vital to me. About as vital to me as the romance Andy and I lacked.

He finished his need for connection and rolled over. We stared at the soft blue light on the ceiling. Silence chilled the heat between us, wrapping us in its bitter wind. I wanted to love him, but our marriage died when he left. He turned over and touched my cheek. His warmth felt like ice cubes on my skin. I jerked away, then apologized. He touched my shoulder instead.

"What's happened to us, bug?" he said, eyes searching my face for clues.

I couldn't tell him that somehow, without being aware of it myself, another man stole my heart and ran away with it. With every part of me I believed my heart was safe. Protected from the care of any man besides Andy. Reserved for when he returned to sweep me off my feet and carry me into a dream. Only he didn't do any sweeping and my heart, somehow, made its way to Patrick's dustpan.

"What are you thinking?" he said. The man I once adored.

"I'm wondering how to get my heart back." I wiped a tear from my face, thankful that I didn't realize my love for Patrick until now. If I had told him this would've been even worse.

"I didn't expect it to be like this," Andy said, moonlight reflecting in the whites of his eyes. "I thought you'd be excited and we'd live happily ever after."

"I did too." I sniffed.

"What happened?"

"Life happened. You are mostly the same guy who left. I'm not the same girl you left standing here."

"I still love you."

Yes, I knew that. For so long I envisioned this day. Thought for sure Andy would come home stronger, less paranoid, more in love with me, brimming and bubbling with romance galore. A new beginning. A beautiful fresh start. A damp spring morning after months of freezing cold.

Nothing seemed beautiful about my life right now. Even my precious daughter brought confusion and pain.

I thought of Tylissa who had a husband facing death penalty and Sarah dealing with pain after burning her entire body. It seemed like a cruel joke. Just when life starts getting good something happens to crush every dream you thought you had. Reality sets in. Waters down the mood. Flattens every romantic notion the heart believed in.

Life is not like the movies. It's not perfect. It's flawed, like a puzzle with missing pieces. Never complete. Never whole. Always searching, climbing, trying to figure out the impossible puzzle of this life, but in the end you're only left with a mess to clean up. Everything seemed unfair.

Why? Why? Why?

In silence, the ever accompanying silence, Andy and I took a bright-eyed baby downstairs to open Christmas gifts. She didn't know what to do with them, except try to eat the paper, so we unwrapped them for her and smiled as she smiled. What a strange Christmas. Andy hadn't left the house since he came back. The only time I left was to get a Christmas tree and groceries.

We tossed all the wrapping paper in a trash bag, then Andy pulled something out of the couch cushions.

"For you." He handed me a small rectangular gift.

"I'm sorry. I have nothing for you. Didn't know you'd be here."

He shook his head. "I didn't get you anything big."

I unwrapped the paper and saw our faces smiling back. Young and excited. "Is this—?"

"It is. The first time you sang the song for me. The one you wrote for your future husband."

I held the faces in my hand. Faces of people I didn't know anymore. "I don't remember taking a picture that night."

"I took a quick one with my camera phone. Quality wasn't as good with that phone, but good enough to have it printed." He stood. "And I have another surprise." He slipped a guitar out from under the couch. "I bought you another guitar. I know how much you loved to play and I always felt bad that we had to sell it to pay the bills, so I bought you another."

I smiled. "Thank you. That's sweet of you." I didn't ask how he made money when he was gone.

"One more surprise." He opened the guitar case. "I learned to play a song. See if you can remember what it is."

I see you smiling there
on the back of my eyes.
And when I open them wide
I see no one in sight.
And I'm looking for the face,
Looking for my love.

Where could he be tonight?
And so I find myself,
Lost and waiting.
Looking for the one
who'll make my dreams come true.

We will walk this life together.
Hand in hand, dreams in tow,

Pulled in a little red wagon
With a little white bow.
We will dance under streetlights.
Kiss beneath the stars.
With a smiling moon above us,
We will disappear together.
Lost in all we have.
Cuz if home is where the heart is,
Then my home is here with you.

And I...
Don't wanna bother you sir,
But could you tell me one thing?
Could you walk this life together
With nothing else but me?
Am I all that you need?

I tried to smile as he set the guitar aside and handed me a frame with the song lyrics inside. I wrote that song for my future husband and sang it to Andy when we first met. The day we believed we finally found our true home in each other as we danced by the crackling fire with hearts in our eyes. We were in love. We were happy.

I kissed him on the cheek and thanked him for learning the song.

He set the guitar down. Stared at me. Waited. For a reaction I couldn't provide.

"I'm sorry," he said. "I really am."

"You are doing the best you can, Andy. I appreciate it."

"But the way you used to look at me. That sparkle in your eyes is gone."

"I know you don't remember because you were so wrapped up in your new job and friends, but that sparkle was gone before you left. It was gone way before the chaos of the life we now live."

"Not like it is now." He sat on the floor with Riley. I couldn't get over his beard and long Axl Rose hair. I'm assuming he felt the need for a disguise. Quite strange.

"I'm trying to adjust," I said. "I think the best thing we can do is start over without pressure. We need to fall in love again. With the people we are now. The longer we spend trying to recapture what we had in the past, the longer we will be frustrated."

He nodded. I sat next to him on the floor. Touched his hand.

"Let's take our rings off," he said. "We'll get new ones when the time is right."

He reached for my hand and slid my rings off with ease, as though the coldness of my heart crept into my hands and made it easier to remove them. A tear slid down my face and stopped on my neck. Then he held his hand for me to do the same.

Hesitant, I pulled back. "Are you sure?"

He nodded. With the same gentle deliberateness that I put his ring on, I took it off. We set them on the table beside us and looked at each other. Absent words. Broken dreams. Nothing left to say except maybe, just maybe, love would fill our hearts again.

If, and only if, I could erase the other man from mine.

Chapter Twelve
Patrick

Maybe to Lancaster with Gavin and Ella. Somewhere. Anywhere but Philly. I needed to get away. The memories in Philly seemed to pile up like a mountain of dog crap. Not exactly the kind of memories you want to cherish.

I called Gavin. "Hey, man. Tell Ella she got her wish."

"What are you talking about?" he said. "Ella is baking cookies for my dad. Do you need her?"

"No, just tell her it looks like I'm going to be faithful to Emily after all."

"Why? I think she was actually rooting for you and Heidi."

"She's like night and day, isn't she? Anyway, tell her to stop rooting. It's not happening. Nothing is happening and I'm going to be single for life."

"What? Are you alright?"

"I'm fine. Slightly enamored with my own misfortune, but fine."

"True love takes work, man. Can't expect everything to be the way you want it to be."

"If love is a game of cards, then I'm the guy who constantly loses."

"It's not that bad."

"It is. Trust me." I sighed. "It's getting ridiculous at this point. I need a break. I'm using some of my savings, going to the airport, and flying who the hell knows where for a few weeks. So if anyone is wondering, that's what happened."

"Anything I can do?"

"Just appreciate what you have with Ella and never let it fade."

"That I can do. See ya soon, Pat. If you need anything we're your people. Oh, and Merry Christmas."

"Yeah, you too."

I hung up, packed a carry-on bag of clothes, toothpaste, and shampoo, and left my apartment for the airport. Figured I'd take the next available flight wherever it went.

I called my secretary in the car and left a message for her to cancel all appointments from now until the second week of January and reschedule them. Also told her to take off and enjoy a vacation.

The airport played holiday tunes as I walked by large Christmas trees lit with cheer. You'd think no one would fly on Christmas, but it was pretty hopping. I scanned the departing flights for something interesting and decided to ask the lady behind the desk to choose for me.

"Anywhere?" she said. "Domestic or international?"

"Anywhere in the U.S."

She pushed a few buttons, charged my card, and smiled as she handed me some papers.

"Have fun," she said.

I nodded, thanked her, and walked away while reading my ticket. Departing in forty-two minutes. Destination? Chicago. Interesting enough. I turned my phone off, checked in, and waited until take off. Felt good to do something for myself for once. Really good, actually.

I SLEPT ON THE PLANE AND DREAMT OF HEIDI. NIGHTMARE central. I woke up with a chill. Something didn't feel right. Brushing emotions aside, I walked off the plane, did all the necessary stuff, and got a rental car. My GPS led me through Chicago. It was late and most of the city was sleeping. Huge beautiful buildings and Christmas lights all over the place. Light dusting of snow, but not enough to cover the city in white. I found a nice hotel by millennium park. The building towered above, lit up like a huge candle glowing in the sky. The valet service took my car and another man ushered me inside. All smiles. I paid for a room and within minutes passed out on the bed. Didn't even take the time to get undressed.

Couldn't sleep though, so I tossed and turned until 5a.m. as I wondered why I spent money to come to a frost-bitten city during Christmas. Should've went to my parents house for turkey and mashed potatoes and dealt with reality.

Once the sun lit the edges of my curtains, I took a shower and got dressed, then found my way to a nice little coffee house by my hotel. Small, but seemed kinda upscale. I paid for a coffee which they made fresh right in front of me, from grinding the beans to a small French press large enough for one cup. Some serious coffee makers, if you ask me.

I sat by the window and scanned the room. One other man about my age sat at the bar reading a newspaper. That's it. Understandable for such an early hour.

I watched people pass. Not many of them did. Still hadn't turned on my phone. And had no plans to. Figured I'd stay a week. Keep my phone off. Process my life. You know, try to relax and then go back to reality when I couldn't avoid it anymore.

I sipped my coffee and noticed a woman sitting by the window across the shop. She looked away when I caught her watching me. I pretended not to notice and pulled a book from my backpack. *The Picture of Dorian Gray* by Oscar Wilde. I scanned the words with my eyes, but my mind kept thinking about Heidi. What was she doing? Was she happy? Who was the guy in her bedroom?

I caught the woman looking at me again. Chestnut hair way passed her shoulders, eyes hiding under long bangs, she would've been worth talking to if I were interested in women.

But I wasn't.

I was interested in singleness for life. It's easier for a woman to get her heart broken in this culture. She gives so much and most men are selfish. But come on now. As a man I had more than my fair share of getting hurt and I wanted nothing to do with the culprit.

Women.

She smiled at me with a pen between her teeth. I'm not dumb. I know flirtatiousness when I see it. So I buried my face behind Dorian Gray and ignored her.

"Excuse me," a gentle voice whispered. "Is this seat taken?"

I peered over the book and shook my head. She sat down. Smiling. I pretended to read.

"I live here," she said. "But you look like you're from somewhere else."

"Philadelphia," I said, not looking up.

"Is it much different there?"

"Not sure. Only been here since last night."

"Oh really? What brings you here for Christmas?"

I put the book on the table and looked into her eyes. "I need a break because women suck the life out of me."

She laughed and put a red beret on her head. "Let's go."

I picked the book back up.

"You're not fooling anyone when you pretend to read that book, you know."

I ignored her and read aloud.

"How old are you?" she said.

"Older than you."

"Today is my birthday. I'm twenty-eight. You look about thirty?"

She crossed her arms and smiled at me as I read. The red beret made her hazel eyes look brown. I couldn't help but notice, although I tried my hardest not to.

"I'm not flirting," she said. "You just look like you could use a friend."

I kept reading. Didn't look up.

"Not all women suck the life out of men. Some of us like to bring life to them. You look like you could use a little resuscitating."

"Not from your mouth," I said.

She laughed. "My name is Nora. It's nice to meet you."

"Why are you spending your birthday talking to a strange man?"

"I need an adventure. This year I promised myself I'd do things I don't normally do. Step one, talk to a complete stranger."

"You seem pretty good at it for a first timer."

A man walked in the door and saw us. "Nora," he said. "Great job with Les Mis. You were incredible as always."

She thanked him and turned back to me. "Let's go," she whispered. "You're not the only one who needs to escape reality."

She stuffed my book into my backpack, took my hand, and pulled me into the blustery morning. Tiny flakes of snow gathered on her red hat as she forced me to run a few city blocks with her.

Out of breath, we stopped at an outdoor ice skating place. Only a few kids messing around. Other than that, just us.

"Ready?" she said.

"For?"

"We're gonna race across the ice. Whoever makes it to the other side first gets to ask the other person a question and they have to answer honestly."

"Nah."

"Come on." She hit my chest. "You're doing it."

Couldn't tell you why I decided to give in. Maybe I needed some adventure too. Maybe I liked her. Maybe, I don't know. I didn't want to think about it, or anything. So I raced her across the ice, slipping and laughing the entire way. We both fell several times before landing safely on the other side. At the exact same time.

"I guess we both get a question." She pulled a blanket from her bag and wrapped it around herself.

"Are we staying outside?"

"For a little."

"But it's freezing. We'll turn into ice sculptures."

She opened up the blanket. "I'll share."

Tempting. "No, thanks. You keep it."

"Okay," she said. "My question first. Describe your heart in three words and then describe why you chose each one."

I thought about it, but the frosty air distracted me. "Can we go back to the coffee shop?"

"Will you answer there?"

I nodded. We stood and made our way back to warmth. I couldn't help but notice her graceful walk. She glazed the city streets with her presence as I walked beside her, hands in my pockets. Her red hat accenting the grey world, a perfect painting in a not-so-perfect world.

We ordered hot chocolates and sat by the window again. A few other people congratulated her on her performance, then she finally asked me to answer her question.

I had some time to think, so I answered quickly. "Lonely, broken, and ready."

She stopped smiling. "Sounds depressing. Why those three?"

Well, why not pour my heart out? Not like I'd ever see the girl again.

"You don't have to answer," she said.

"Lonely because my wife died before she ever learned to love me. Broken because the only other woman I allowed myself to love is sleeping with another man. And ready because I'm more than ready to move on with life and be happy again, without the help of a woman."

She thought for a minute. "Well, it was a tie. So what do you want to ask me?"

"Same thing, I guess."

"Broken, artificial, and hopeful."

"Okay. Why?"

"Like you, unrequited love has a way of breaking hearts. Artificial because I'm pretty and people have always focused too much on my looks and not enough on who I am. Which means men want only my body and women hate me. Hopeful because I'm exhausted. I give myself constantly to others either on stage or in life, and well, it can only get better from here, right?"

"I know a few guys back home who wouldn't look at you that way. In fact, I also know a guy who proposed to a gorgeous girl. Right after that they had a campfire accident and I doubt she will ever be physically gorgeous again."

"Wow." She picked apart a straw wrapper and played with the pieces on the table. "Did he stay with her?"

"Barely leaves her side to eat."

"So why is the woman you fell in love with sleeping with another man?"

"I definitely don't want to talk about that right now." I wrapped my hands around my cold hot chocolate mug, wishing it were still warm. "Why don't you tell me all about your depressing love story instead?"

"I'm an open book. Just a few pages glued together here and there."

"So what happened?"

"Not sure. Greyson isn't ready for marriage. I am. Different ideals and dreams, I guess. He is more into money and having a nice looking girl around his arm. I'm not like that."

"Then why do you love him?"

"We've known each other since elementary school. Best friends through fifth grade. We never told each other we had crushes and then he moved away. His parents got divorced and his mom took him to Wisconsin. We lost touch until he came back here for college. I walked into my first class in college and sat next to him. No other seats in the class. We didn't recognize each other at first, but I saw his name on his paper and the rest is history. We've been together on and off for almost a decade. Now we're off again."

"Yeah."

She laughed. "Profound response."

"I'm all out of deep today."

"Anyway, people change. The boy I fell in love with twenty years ago is not the man I want to spend my life with."

I liked her. Not in a romantic way. Refused to let my heart go there. But I liked her personality. Couldn't understand why on earth a guy would choose anything over her, but to each his own.

"So," she said. "I better get going. I have an audition to prepare for. Actually trying to make my way to New York."

"Broadway?"

"Hoping."

"Thought you didn't want that kind of life?"

"Nothing else to do. I won't let the fame get to my head." She laughed. "Doubt they will accept me anyway." She stuck out her hand. I shook. "Nice meeting you. What's your name?"

"Patrick."

She stood. Something mysterious and intriguing about her smile. "Goodbye then, Patrick."

I watched her skip down the street with one hand on her hat. Yes, skip. She crossed the street, stood on her toes, and waved to me. I waved back, laughed. Weird girl, I thought. Very weird.

Chapter Thirteen
Heidi

New Years Eve I opened my eyes in bed. Andy packed most of our essentials and told me to be ready to leave for another country by New Years Eve. So I was.

Riley slept passed her normal time. I rolled over to wake Andy with a kiss before the baby would steal my attention, but he wasn't there. He always woke up before me. Since the day I met him. He called me his little night owl and I called him my early birdie. We had so many cutesie names for each other. Enough to sicken the average person.

I closed my eyes and listened for the shower. Didn't hear a thing. Patrick. I needed to tell him the truth. He deserved to know. Except Andy didn't want anyone knowing he was still alive, not even his parents. He believed some crazy gang was out to get him. I loved him, so I kept his secrets. At the very least I needed to tell Patrick that I loved him, but I would be moving away and he needed to move on.

My stomach turned. I sat up. Nauseous at the idea of never speaking to Patrick again. His smile. The way he fought for me and waited for me. Not once did he try to kiss me, even when I desperately wanted him to. The way he respected me and loved me from a distance, no matter how much he wanted to be with me. Andy was the wall between us, and crazy as it sounded, Patrick stayed on the other side. He became my best friend. The best one I ever had. And as much as I wanted to believe in my marriage, my heart really resided in my best friends hands.

But I needed to be faithful. Andy was a good guy too. I couldn't break his heart.

After checking on Riley, I went downstairs. No sign of Andy. I walked to the front door and saw a note on the table by the couch. Andy's writing in scratches of blue ink.

> *They are after me again. I don't want you to get hurt. Burn this note and live without me again. It won't be long. Just until they forget again. Next time I come back be ready to leave with me right away. Keep a bag packed in case. I will come back for you, bug. Don't forget me. So sorry about this mess.*

The first time he left I balled like a baby. Took me two days to get out of bed and eat again. This time I sighed, annoyed. What did he expect from me? From Riley? We needed stability, and although I didn't need it to survive, I wanted romance. I wanted true love.

Andy feared death. I feared living my life without love. Death didn't scare me, but a life unlived scared me a lot.

I texted Miranda to see what her New Years plans were. She replied within minutes. A gathering at Matt and Lydia's. I bet Patrick would be there. Would be weird seeing him again. Especially since not talking to him in a while.

Will Pat be there? I texted.

Thought you knew? He's in Chicago until Monday. Been there since Christmas.

We haven't talked. I will be there. See ya then.

I wanted to call Andy and tell him to come back and deal with life, but he refused to own a cell phone. He said they—not sure who "they" were—would listen to his calls and track his location. Last time he left he never contacted me. Not once. Not until his bearded face came back home and expected me to pretend like he never left.

I got Riley out of bed and looked at her leg. Poor thing should've been walking, or trying to, but her leg was about an inch shorter than the other one, maybe a little more. She tried to creep around furniture but I wouldn't let her. I didn't want her to cause any more problems. Doctor said it was okay, but I couldn't help worrying.

"Hey, sweetie," I said. "Your birthday is coming in a few days."

She smiled and babbled. No daddy to celebrate her first birthday with her. He probably didn't even know her birthday.

But Patrick did.

Chapter Fourteen
Patrick

New Years Eve in a big city and no plans. I liked it that way. After a long shower I settled under the blankets of the stiff hotel bed and opened my book again. Four pages into chapter fifteen and blue ink caught my attention. *Nora Madison. 610-555-8834. Call if you're bored.*

I hadn't turned on my phone since I left. Didn't want to see a thousand emails and texts pop up. So I ignored the blue ink and kept reading until the curiosity sparked my fingers and I dug my phone out of my backpack.

I ignored the text and email notifications and dialed her number. Her voicemail picked up and I left a message. Five minutes later the phone rang.

"Hey, Patrick," she said. "You looking for something to do later tonight?"

"I guess. I'm actually heading back tomorrow. Earlier than I thought so I can get back to work. Do you have New Years plans?"

"Now I do. Meet me at the ice skating park in thirty minutes."

I hung up the phone and wondered if it's really possible for a man to be "just friends" with an extremely attractive woman. The answer is no. At least for me. So what the hell was I thinking?

Not thinking. That's what I was doing. And that's what I did as I walked through cold air to the ice skating park, which was a hundred times busier. I sat on a bench and watched love skate by. Five hundred times. Couples holding hands, gazing into each others eyes, making me sick to my stomach.

"Boo." A figure popped out from under the bench.

I yelled and jumped out of my seat. Nora laughed, half of her body still under the bench.

I held my chest. "That's not even right."

She stopped laughing. "Couldn't help myself. You looked deep in thought."

"No, just analyzing the couples skating by."

She stood in front of me. Hands at her sides. Hair curled down to her elbows. Cream scarf wrapped around her neck and tucked into her red coat. No hat this time.

"You have a thing for red?" I said, trying not to look into her eyes.

"Favorite color to wear."

"What's your favorite color not-to-wear?"

She grabbed my coat and pressed her peppermint lips against mine. My heart, breaking in half, pulled away, but my lips stayed on hers. I kissed her back. Without my heart. And I hated every second of it.

She sat on the bench. "That was a test."

"Huh?" I said.

"I failed." She pointed to me. "But you passed."

"I'm not good with riddles." I sat beside her.

"I wanted to see if I kissed this super attractive guy with one of the sweetest personalities I've ever known, if I'd think of Greyson." She smiled. "Good news. I didn't think of him at all. I think I'm finally over him." She pointed to me again. "But your heart is still with someone else. I could tell."

"My heart is in the trash can."

She laughed. I couldn't help but laugh too.

"I'm serious," I said.

"How melodramatic of you to be so serious."

I tilted my head back and looked at the stars. She did the same.

"I've been reading Oscar Wilde lately. He says, 'We are all in the gutter, but some of us are looking at the stars.' I guess I can see what he's saying."

"And Shakespeare says, 'It's not in the stars to hold our destiny, but in ourselves.'"

"I wonder what that means."

"I think it means we have a say in the story of our lives."

I nodded. Imagined Heidi. Imagined going back home and talking to her again. Telling her what I heard. I loved that girl so much that part of me wanted to ignore it and love her anyway, but I couldn't. Not after everything with Emily. I wanted a normal relationship. I wanted someone who didn't sleep around.

"You're thinking about her, aren't you?" Nora pulled her knees to her chest and faced me.

I nodded. "I'm always thinking about her."

"Why are you sitting here then?"

"Because she is probably sitting with another man."

"Go." She stood. "I mean it. Go right now. "

I laughed. "You remind me of my friend Ella."

"She sounds nice."

I laughed again. "She is."

She tugged my coat. "Go get your backpack and leave. Where do you live again?"

"Philadelphia."

"Okay. Meet me at the airport in twenty minutes. I'm gonna grab some clothes."

"What?"

"I'm coming with you."

"Why?"

"Why did you come to Chicago?"

"To get away. Take a break."

"Same here. I've never been to Philadelphia. So, thanks for inviting me."

I smiled. "You're a weird one."

She spun around with a smile, then skipped off, turning once to shout, "Twenty minutes. Don't be late."

NORA TOOK THE WINDOW SEAT AND I SAT BESIDE HER. ONLY a handful of passengers on the plane. There were more on Christmas than New Years, which I found strange.

She took off her coat and made herself comfortable. We barely talked the entire way.

As the plane landed she finally turned to me. "So, your friends doing anything special tonight? It's about an hour till the ball drops."

"They're all at my friend Matt's house."

"Will she be there?"

"Doubt it. She's taking a break from everyone right now." I looked at my phone. "I would've gotten a text or call from her if she wanted to see me again."

"Why isn't she talking to you?"

"She said she needed some time to think."

We didn't say another word until I parked in front of Matt's house.

"This is Philly?" she said.

"Are you disappointed?"

"I thought we'd see the city."

"Meet some people tonight and you'll find your way around town. You can probably stay with Miranda or Dee. They'll give you a tour."

"What about you?"

"What about me?"

"We're friends, right?"

"I guess."

She laughed. "Such enthusiasm."

I knocked on the door. No answer. Too loud inside. We walked in and I introduced Nora to Matt and Miranda. They made her feel comfortable as they always did with new people. Then I scanned the room. Pregnant Lydia next to Dee. A group of guys I met once before. Probably Dee's friends. Couldn't remember their names. Some girls Lydia went to school with, Myra being one of them.

Gavin and Ella gave me a hug.

"How was your trip?" Gavin said.

Before I could answer Ella introduced her brother. "Have you met my brother Derek yet?"

"At the wedding." I shook his hand. "Nice seeing you again."

"You too," he said. "I'm thinking of moving here from Virginia."

"Oh yeah?" I smiled. "How's that going?"

"Who knows."

I looked at Ella. "So what's new? What did I miss?"

"Not much. Sarah is doing well. Her recovery is going a lot better than the doctors anticipated. She hides her emotions though. Kills me when she doesn't open up, but hopefully she does with James. He's doing really well. Tylissa is a wreck. We may have her move in with us because she is having a tough time paying the bills. Um." She looked at Gavin. "What else?"

He continued for her. "We announced our pregnancy to everyone tonight. Other than that, can't think of anything new."

"Who's the girl you brought?" Ella said.

"Met her in Chicago. She's a little crazy, but nice. Maybe you can play Cupid tonight. She could use a nice man."

Ella'a face glowed. "Maybe Griffin. He's a little strange on the surface too, but very deep and reflective."

"Have at it." I laughed.

"Did you come here to see Heidi?" Gavin said. "She'll definitely be surprised."

"She's here?"

"You didn't know?"

I shook my head. "Where is she?"

"Upstairs feeding the baby."

My heart didn't hesitate, so my body followed it upstairs. I heard sniffing from a bedroom and walked right in. Heidi turned. Glassy eyes filled with pain. My hands shook as my vision muddied. Standing there, clutching my hands together, I gave her whatever was left of me.

"Heidi." My lip wouldn't stop shaking. "Listen to me, I love you. Okay? I can't do this. My heart is all knotted up in you and it feels like I'm dying when we don't talk. These last few weeks have been the worst of my life. I can't live without you. I'd rather die."

Her tears covered her lips. She tried to speak, but couldn't. I moved toward her, touched her face, wanted to kiss her with every part of my existence. I looked down and took her hand. "Please, Heidi. Please let me love you."

She covered her face with her arm and sobbed. Riley sat on the floor below us, staring up at me like nothing was wrong. I picked her up, kissed her, and set her back down.

"Some love stories don't make sense. Stop trying to make it make sense. This is us. We are meant for each other. I don't give a damn if I had to marry five people to discover the right one, but here I am. I made mistakes. I married for the wrong reasons and I was willing to devote my life to her. But she's gone. Andy and Emily are gone. It's us. Me and you. And it may

not be your typical Hollywood chick flick, but we are meant for each other."
I noticed Heidi's bare hand. No rings. "Please say something. Tell me why
you are crying."

She wiped her tears away and looked up at me, face still wet and flushed.
"Pat." She held back tears again, then said, "Patrick, I love you more than I
ever thought I could love another person, but I can't—" She grabbed Riley
and ran out the door, sobbing again.

I stood there. Rejected. Again. For who knows what reason.

I ran down the steps and through the crowd as they yelled "Happy
New Year." With confetti flying at my face, I opened the front door and
pleaded with my entire body for her to wait. To come back. To tell me what
I said wrong.

She started her car and pulled away. From the middle of the street, out
of breath and life, I yelled into the wintry air, "I love you." Her car lights
disappeared into the night and took my heart for the ride. Happy New Year.

My friends stood on the lawn, waiting for me to come back, most likely
wondering if I had lost my mind. No, no, not the mind, I whispered inside.
Just the heart.

Chapter Fifteen
Heidi

Shattered. His face. Standing in front of me with tears hidden beneath his eyes. His heart. Spread out on the floor and ready for love. For me. For us.

It killed me. Ruined me. Like a paper ripped into a million tiny pieces and tossed into the sea. Washed away. Disintegrated. I drove away. I had no choice. Tears washed my face as Riley cried in the backseat. In my rearview mirror Patrick's tired silhouette faded into a shadow in the night, clouded by my tears.

I love you, Patrick, I thought inside, trying not to convulse, trying to steer the car without crashing. I loved him so much. So, so much more than I ever thought I could love another man after everything I'd endured with Andy. More than passion and long talks. More than cozy movie nights and best friends. More than anything he could ever give me. I loved him because I couldn't help myself. Period. Reasonable or not, I loved him.

Dear Juliet. I could relate to her pain. Black misery painted on a blood red heart. Death would be more bearable than life without Romeo.

I parked in front of my house. A figure moved in the vacant house across the street. For sale sign had been gone for weeks. I didn't care tonight. My heart was beating, but only physically.

I needed to be strong for Riley, but I collapsed on my front lawn with her. Sobbing and drenching her with my broken heart, my incurable love and hopeless dreams.

A shadow hovered beside us. I jumped up, hugging Riley to my chest as she cried. Some kind of animal scurried off as I hurried to my house and opened the door, then locked it.

For a few minutes I stood there, breathing heavy and wishing for things

I couldn't have. For things to be different. I wished Andy had never left the first time, then I wouldn't have fallen in love with Patrick. And now he left again, hoping I'd wait around with a messed up heart.

I put Riley to sleep and sauntered into my bedroom around 1a.m. The bed hadn't been made from yesterday. Not typical for me. I climbed inside and felt a warm body.

Tucked under the blankets, Andy slept. Back again. So soon. I tugged his shoulder until he woke.

"Where were you?" he said without opening his eyes.

"A friends house." I pulled the blankets to my chin and stared at the ceiling. "Andy, I want to leave with you next time. No more notes and random disappearances. Take me with you. I can't stay here."

He opened his eyes. "What about Riley?"

"I'll just have to come back to Baltimore when she needs her surgeries. First one is this spring."

"I can't get on a plane. They are watching us. We will have to drive somewhere and ditch the car when we get there. We can live in the woods and I will hunt for our food."

I turned to him. "I'm not doing that. Not with Riley."

"It's the only choice. That or death."

I didn't believe him. Didn't believe any part of his strange stories. He took it too far. "You know what?" I said. "Some people would rather die than be without the person they love, but you have no problem leaving me for months at a time because you don't want to die."

"It's also because I don't want you to die." He flung out of bed and ran to the window. "Duck, duck. Hurry."

I rolled off the bed to the floor. Waited.

"They're here," he whispered. "Don't you hear the gun shots? They're coming."

"I didn't hear gun shots."

"Shhh. They'll hear you."

I stood and walked to the window. Andy pulled me to the ground.

"Are you crazy?" he said. "They'll shoot you. Stay down."

His hands trembled in the moonlight. I grabbed them. Held them.

"Andy, I can't do this anymore."

He put his hand over my mouth. "Quiet."

I ripped his hand off. "I'm not doing this anymore. I don't hear gun shots. There's no one after us. Even if they were, I. Don't. Care. I'm not living like this anymore."

He fell to the ground and held his ears. "Watch out," he screamed.

I stood. "They're here. They're here. Andy, we need to find a safe place. Let's hide."

He stood. "You saw them?"

I pointed out the window. "There's no one here."

"They were. I heard the gun shots."

"Andy, maybe you need to go get some help at the hospital."

"No."

"I'm serio—"

"No." His tone raised a few notches, but he quickly calmed down. "You don't believe me, do you? You think I'm crazy."

"What do you want from me? Since that job promotion and that stupid banking scandal you've went nuts. Talking about gangs and drones and poison in the water. You're afraid to die, yes, that's apparent. But you're also afraid to live."

He paced the dark room. "You don't understand."

"I don't. That's true. But can you try to understand me? Where I'm coming from? I have a baby who needs major medical treatment and a husband who keeps disappearing, changing his appearance, and coming back only to leave again. He tells me to pretend like he's dead. To lie to everyone including his parents. And then he wants me to take my baby and run away with him to some unknown place because he fears death."

"First of all, she's not your baby. She's ours. Second of all, if you believed me you'd understand why I'm doing this. It's not out of fear, Heidi. It's out of love for you and Riley. I don't want you to get hurt."

"You're already hurting me, Andy." I shook the tears away. "Don't you see? You're killing everything that was ever good in me. My hope. My heart. It's all dying."

"Maybe I should just go."

"That doesn't solve the problem."

"I will leave you alone forever." He walked toward the door.

"Andy." I touched his shoulder. "Don't run from life. Or death. Just relax and live."

He sat on the bed, slumped over. "But you don't believe me. You just think I'm crazy."

"It doesn't matter what I think." I sighed. "How about we move to Maryland? Or Virginia? Somewhere close to Riley's doctors. We can start over."

"I'll need to go by a different name from now on, and be your brother or boyfriend or something. Otherwise it's too obvious."

I sat beside him and touched his face. How could I leave him? No matter how much Patrick loved me, Andy needed me. He needed someone to hug him. To tell him it would be okay. To try to make him better. Patrick wanted me, but my husband needed me, I told myself, over and over, as I stroked Andy's unwashed hair.

Sure, it wasn't a fairy tale, but if I valued emotions more than faithfulness and virtue, what kind of person would I be? It wouldn't be fair to Andy or Patrick. Or myself. I longed to see Andy recover from this horrible period of life and truly open his eyes to life again. What a day it would be to see the man I married smile again. Really smile.

Faithfulness, true and faithful love, never has limits. It will do whatever it takes, sacrifice all its desires, to see another person smile. That's what I needed to do.

My desires, my hope, my love for Patrick, it all needed to die so Andy could live again.

Chapter Sixteen
Patrick

The heart has its limits. I could endure a lot. Plenty more than most men. All I wanted was honesty. Why couldn't she love me? And why did she take her rings off? Did she fall in love with someone else?

I wanted answers. That's it. She didn't want me, fine. But at least give me a reason.

I drove to her house and set her gift against the front door, then drove away. Miserable.

Right before going to sleep I texted her. One last time. *I love you, sweet one. Goodnight.* Then I zonked out and woke up at noon the next day to my phone beeping. A text from Nora. I rolled over and went back to sleep until 1p.m.

I dreamt of Emily and woke up believing she was still alive, so I decided to visit her grave. Heidi most likely found the gift and made her choice.

I checked my phone when I got out of the shower. Nothing from Heidi. Just Nora thanking me—in sixteen texts—for bringing her to Philly. She loved the city. Miranda showed her around. I knew they'd get along. Both weird people. In a nice way, I mean. I think.

By the time I got to Emily's grave the sun settled behind the trees, one last burst of light before dark. I sat in front of the stone and stared at the name of the girl that was born Emily Dalton and died with my last name. Poor soul. Never had the chance to live. Spent the first half of her life abused and the last half wishing she were never born.

"I wonder if you can hear me, Em." I ran my fingers along the letters on the stone as the sun said goodnight and left me in the cold. "I'm sorry I couldn't give you the life you always dreamed of. You were just a little girl.

I thought I could help you and fell in love with you in the process. Looking back, Em, I think I just fell in love with being your savior. Something I was never meant to be. I couldn't be. You never gave me a chance to know you." I stood. "I'm moving on now. I hope you understand. My heart is finally broken. It can't handle anymore. I'm walking away tonight, Em. I'll take your memory with me, but I'm starting over, rebuilding the heart I lost. I'm gonna build it into something new. I hope you are smiling down on me. I hope you're better now."

I pulled a picture of her from my wallet. Edges worn, color faded. It was the last picture of her before she lost all of her hair. Slight smile. Wind blown hair. Eyes on the camera, not on me.

I placed it in front of her gravestone. "Goodbye, Emily."

THE NEXT MORNING I WENT TO WORK HOPING TO FEEL renewed after the final goodbye to my past. Instead, I checked my phone five thousand times for a message from Heidi. I didn't feel refreshed or rebuilt. I needed the love of my life to help me rebuild my life. There's no way I could've imagined my life without her. Can't even explain it. Sometimes people enter your heart like Gavin and Ella. Love at first sight, all dramatic and movie-like. Other times people enter your heart through friendship, slipping through the cracks like a flower in the midst of concrete slabs. That was Heidi and me. Somehow the seed fell into the fractured sidewalk and without knowing, love grew.

But . . . when most people find a flower growing from the sidewalk they step on it or yank it out like a weed. It's not normal. Not allowed. Like our love.

I needed to let her go.

I plowed through clients and decided to meet the guys for dinner. Absolutely no talking about Heidi. I warned them ahead of time. Time for me to pretend like my heart wasn't hers. The better I pretended, perhaps the more real it would become.

I met Gavin, Matt, Reese, James, and my old buddy from high school, Julian, at a local joint outside of Philly that served amazing local food alongside their specialty beer. Loved the atmosphere, and especially the bread and butter, so I requested the place. Everyone obliged and Gavin even traveled from Lancaster.

I got there first, reserved a table by the exposed brick wall, and waited for everyone to show up. Already ordered water and bread. Had a slice as I waited. Delicious. I mean, phenomenal. Never had anything like it before. They made their bread in-house. Crispy, but airy inside, dipped in a creamy pile of salted butter from a local farm. Seriously loved Pennsylvania for its farms and local produce. I ate a second slice as Julian walked in and spotted me. I waved him over and he sat down beside me, shook my hand and hit my back.

"Hey, man," he said. "Been a year since I've seen you. How you been?"

"Been better, but I'm here to try not to think about it. So tell me about your life."

"Ah, man, I ain't got much good to say either. Life's been crazy for me. Ain't had much time to breath. Shit's been hitting the fan like there ain't no tomorrow."

"Why? What's going on?"

"I got involved with the wrong crowd. Hard to find a job, man. I don't know. I'm tired of life. Need a break."

"I hear ya."

Gavin and Matt walked over and sat down, followed by Reese and James. Within minutes we ordered three more rounds of bread. They liked it too. Anyone would.

"How's Sarah?" I said to James after swallowing another bite.

"Okay, I guess. She's handling it better than I am, but she doesn't have to deal with the guilt I have. Thank God. Last thing she needs."

"Do they know when she'll come home?"

"Maybe by summer if all goes as planned. Hard to say. It sucks, dude. Seriously. Worst thing I ever endured. Seeing her like that. Her entire body is one big scar. My scars are all underneath my shirt and it's not that bad. She hasn't seen a mirror yet, but she says she would rather live without beauty than die beautiful. She told me real beauty doesn't ever rot in a casket. It lives forever. She thinks she's been given a second chance to gain this real beauty thing, but she already had that too. It's not just her looks though, the girl's gonna be suffering for years with surgeries and skin grafts and infections." He exhaled and picked up his water. "Anyway, enough depressing talk. We came here to enjoy ourselves. Sorry to vent."

"Nah, man," Julian said. "Don't apologize. We all got our problems. Life ain't life unless it's got conflict."

"True," Matt said, raising his glass. "The best stories in the world are so amazing because in the end the goal was worth the struggle."

"Yeah," Gavin said. "If it's not worth fighting for then the story ends. There is no story without a fight."

"What if you give up?" I said, another huge slice of bread in my hand.

"Then there's no more story," Gavin said. "Maybe you stop reading and pick up another book."

"What if every book you find reminds you of the first one, but doesn't come close to touching its beauty? Do you go back and finish the other story? Or allow a new story to become better than the one you can't forget?"

"What the?" Matt said. "Speak in English. What are you trying to say?"

I shrugged. "Never mind."

"Nothing will ever be better," Reese chimed in. "Just different. You are the only one who can decide which story is worth the obstacles." He looked around the table. "Myra is back home now. She overstayed her visa. Now there's no way I can see her unless I go to the Philippines. And I can't become a citizen there easily. It's a mess. Finally find everything you want and it's stolen from you and shipped across the world."

"Isn't there anything you can do?" I said.

"I'm looking into it. You better believe I'll fight like hell through these obstacles for her. She's definitely worth it and I'm not interested in a different story, no matter how hard this one is right now."

Wow. I listened to the guys talk about their own obstacles until the conversation lightened up and shifted gears toward which decade had the best music. I didn't talk much the rest of the night. Listened. Wondered. Checked my phone every once in a while hoping for some sort of closure from Heidi. Anything. Anything at all.

But I got nothing.

Chapter Seventeen
Heidi

A ndy and I decided to move to Maryland. Not too far from Riley's doctors. He told me to continue my business from home when I got to our new apartment, and we'd worry about selling the house on weekends. We'd live close enough that I could drive back and work with a realtor.

Honestly, I didn't feel like I had a choice. As a married woman, I needed to stick by my husband. For better or worse.

He took a shower as I put Riley to sleep. We hadn't left the house since New Years, so he told me to run out for some food and he would stay with the baby. When I opened the door a package fell on my feet. Pink and silver stripes.

I picked it up and sat on the couch, then slipped the wrapping paper off and stared at the cover of a deep red scrapbook with the title, "The Story of Us."

I flipped to the first page. Two broken hearts pasted next to each other. One said "Heidi" above it and the other said "Patrick." I wiped my eyes and turned the page. A drawing of Patrick and I racing each other down the street. The note above it said, "The first night I realized I couldn't live without you, even if it meant never being yours." I read the rest of the book, reliving memories with Patrick and realizing how beautiful our time together was. No sex. No kissing. No passionate heated embraces. We were best friends. We loved each other inside out.

I turned to the last page. A fork in the road with him on one side and a question mark on the other. The note said: *Both paths lead to the unknown. We can never know what tomorrow brings. But if you choose the first path we will walk this life together. We will face the unknown in each others arms. If you choose the second path you will face the unknown without me. I've left the rest of the pages in this scrapbook blank, in hopes that one day we can fill the rest together. If you love me, just tell me and we will start our life together. I am nothing without you. I love you, butter.*

I tried not to cry, but couldn't help it. Andy rustled upstairs. I hid the book under the couch cushions and went upstairs.

"Hey," I said to Andy. "Can we order a pizza? I don't feel like going out right now."

"You okay?" he said. "Looks like you've been crying."

"Pizza okay?"

"Sure."

"I'll go order it."

I went to the kitchen and pulled my phone from the charger. Two missed text messages. Pat. *I can't do this. I'm trying to let you go, but I don't think I can unless I'm dead. Heidi, please tell me how you feel.*

I thought for a minute. All cried out. Ignoring his text, I ordered a pizza and sat at the kitchen table. Another text from him. *You there?*

I typed back. *Pat, this is the hardest thing I've ever done in my life. I can't tell you why, but I'm moving. Please let me go. We can't be together.*

I waited. Ashamed to hit send. Ashamed to choose the path without him. Didn't want to break his heart. He had been through so much with Emily. I so longed to love him the way he deserved. But I couldn't. I shouldn't have led him on in the first place.

I hit send.

A single tear landed on the kitchen table. Next to my phone. I waited for him to respond, but he never did.

Pizza came. Andy walked downstairs, smiling. He hugged me and sat down at the table. In anxiety disguised by quiet peace, we ate dinner.

"You look like you've lost weight," I said. "Are you okay?"

"I feel fine," he said.

We finished eating and spent the rest of the evening watching a Julia Roberts movie.

I fell asleep and when I woke at 3a.m. Andy was still watching movies.

"Can't sleep," he said. "It's not fear. I just haven't been able to sleep right lately."

"I will call and find an apartment in Maryland tomorrow. Once I secure one we will move."

"No. We need to move tomorrow. We can't stay here. They'll kill us."

I yawned. "Come upstairs with me. We can talk about it tomorrow."

He turned the television off and scanned the front yard before following me up the stairs. I sighed.

The next few hours I barely slept as Andy tossed and turned, grunting and moaning, unable to sleep. His body was covered in sweat even without blankets and at random moments it looked like he was combing his hair in his sleep.

I tapped him at 6a.m. "You okay?"

He shot out of bed and ran to the window. "Where are they?"

"Who?"

"Did you hear that?"

"Andy," I said. "We need to talk. I need to be honest with you about something."

"I know you think I'm crazy. I'm not, Heidi. You have to believe me. You of all people."

"It's not that. It's about a guy I met when you were away."

Chapter Eighteen
Patrick

I never believed I was a hero, so I didn't pretend to be one. She wanted me to let her go, so I did. At least physically. I wouldn't call or text or try to see her. Not unless she wanted to. I know women say things they don't mean sometimes. When they want you to stay they tell you to go away. It's a game, really. A test to see if the man loves her enough to stay even when she begs him to leave. My grandfather once told me, "Always go after the girl. No matter what she says. Chase her."

I understood that. Sounds wonderful. Sounds romantic. But I did my chasing and she obviously meant what she said. She didn't want me in her life. Maybe it was too hard to let go of Andy. Maybe she fell in love with me and hated that she did.

I didn't want that for her. All I wanted was to see her smile. So I let her go, as she wished.

A few days passed and I got used to the idea. I finally walked away from my past and I needed to toss my memories of Heidi into that bin too. The bin of cast away dreams.

Gavin convinced me that I'd find someone for me. Someone who completed me. Thing is . . . I wasn't looking for completion or romance or lovey-dovey hand holding in the park. In fact, I wasn't looking for anything. She showed up and stole my heart and my life wouldn't be the same without her. I didn't want a wife, completion, whatever. I wanted Heidi.

I stayed late in my office. Staring at my computer screen. My secretary left hours before. I couldn't move. Nothing to do. Nowhere to be. Bored out of my mind.

I skimmed the contact list in my phone and settled on Miranda.

"Hey, Patrick," she said. "How's everything going?"

"It's going nowhere. What are you up to?"

"Nothing much. Derek just left for Virginia, thankfully. About to lose my mind with his unwanted opinions on everything. Nora is still here. She's leaving tomorrow."

"You two weirdos getting along?"

"Yeah." She laughed. "Couldn't convince her to dye her hair purple though."

"Good."

"What? You don't like my multi-colored locks?"

"No. Definitely prefer normal women, but that's okay. You have Derek."

"I don't have Derek and he certainly doesn't have me."

"Yeah. You're just too busy looking at the world around you to notice."

"I'm not ready to settle down. Anyway, what's on your mind tonight? Need something? Highly unlike you to call someone as normal as me."

I almost laughed. "How's Heidi?"

"I wish I knew. She hasn't talked to me since New Years Eve. Ignores my texts. I stopped by her house the other night to make sure she was okay. Saw the light on upstairs so I assumed she just needed space."

"Why would she ignore you too?"

"No idea. Hopefully it's just a phase."

"She sent me a vague text. Said she's moving. Any idea why or where?"

"Nope. Never said anything to me about it."

"I don't get it."

"Why don't you go over there? Knock on the door and make her talk to you."

"I'm not that kind of guy."

"What's that supposed to mean?"

"I'm not just going to show up."

"Maybe that's what she needs."

I hung up with Miranda and an email popped up on my computer. Looked like spam, but I accidentally opened it instead of deleting it.

From: Secret Admirer
To: Patrick Weldon
Subject: Here goes nothing

Dear Patrick,

I'm not going to tell you who I am. Not yet at least. I was told you are going through some heartbreak because of a girl who doesn't love you the way you love her. I was also told that you wouldn't want to talk to me because of that, so I thought I'd email you instead. I got your email from a mutual friend. Don't try to guess who.

I'm writing because I saw you at a New Years party at Matt and Lydia's house. You didn't notice me because of the girl you were after, but I noticed you.

Maybe it's weird, but it was love at first sight for me. The first time I saw you I knew I could spend the rest of my life with you. I think if you saw me it would be mutual.

Let me know if you'd be willing to meet me. I'd love to get to know you. Maybe we could talk on the phone first?

Love,
Your One True Love

I immediately called Matt.

"Who put you up to this?" I said. "I'm not falling for your dumb pranks. It's not funny."

"Whoa," Matt said. "Calm down. What are you talking about?"

"My secret admirer. I know this is a prank. I'm not stupid."

"Seriously have no idea what you're talking about, dude."

"I got an email from an address patrickwheldonsgirl@gmail.com who claims to be a girl from your party at New Years. She's claiming we are destined for each other."

He laughed. "I'm not a part of this. Sounds interesting though. What did she say?"

"Wants to meet up or talk on the phone. Saw me at the party. Were there girls at your house I hadn't met before?"

"Let me think." He paused for a few seconds. "There were a few. Myra brought another girl from the Philippines. Super beautiful and she was very quiet and nice. Then there was another girl. I think she was a friend of Miranda. Other than that and the girl you brought, I have no idea."

"This better not be a prank."

"Why? Do you like having a secret admirer?"

"I'm just not in the mood for games."

"I'd say meet her. Can't hurt to go on a date."

"Do you remember how those blind dates turned out for you?"

He laughed.

"Yeah, not interested."

We ended our conversation and I stared at the email. Spam wouldn't have had all the references to Matt's house. I hit reply.

From: Patrick Wheldon
To: Secret Admirer
Subject: RE: Here goes nothing

Dear person, if you are a real person,

I'm sorry to seem so rude, but I have no interest in dating right now. I'm sure you are a wonderful person and would make a great wife, but you won't be my wife. Find a man who can love you right. Don't chase after me because I'm heartbroken. Why do girls do that anyway? You can't save me. No one will compare to the one I love. If I can't have her, I don't want anyone else. I hope you don't take it personal, but my heart belongs to her. Always will.

I hope you find someone better than what I can give. And I'm sure you will, because I have nothing to give.

Patrick

From: Secret Admirer
To: Patrick Wheldon
Subject: RE: Here goes nothing

I understand. Could we just be friends? Wanna meet me at Starbucks tonight at 7pm? If not, maybe we could just email. I could use a friend right now.

I responded and told her I'd email, but nothing else. Didn't want to give her any ideas or false hopes. Being heartbroken is contagious and I didn't want to see anyone as sick as me.

Chapter Nineteen
Heidi

I tried to tell Andy about Patrick, but he said, "If you didn't kiss or have sex with him, I don't care. I'm back now and I know you love me." I did love him, of course. But things changed. Now I loved him because he needed me, not because I couldn't imagine my life without him. I could imagine it, because it happened.

We packed a few suitcases and loaded up my car. Andy wanted to leave first thing in the morning. He thought "they" wouldn't be watching if we left earlier. I agreed so long as we could take my car.

We left at sunrise. Riley played in the backseat as we drove off in silence. I left a message on a realtors phone the night before. Hopefully I'd have no problems selling the place.

Andy didn't have a destination. We drove south and he said we'd know when we found our new home, just like we knew we were home when we found each other. I tried to smile. Tried to resurrect my feelings for him, but the love I had for him was different now. Less romantic and more sacrificial. Maybe that's true love, I thought to myself. When you love someone more than yourself, more than your own hopes and dreams.

Movies and books accentuated sensualism and romanticism. I never liked that. Almost boycotted it most of my life. Probably because it made me feel inadequate, like my dreams could never be attained and I'd live my life depressed because of it. I let go of my hopes for the perfect love story, but couldn't it be just as beautiful to stay faithful to someone your entire life even when emotions are absent? Emotions come and go, it's how much we love when they go that shows what kind of person we really are.

I didn't want to be selfish. Andy was a good guy. He loved me as much as he could love a person. It may not had been the love story of my dreams, but the beauty of some love stories isn't so much in the highs as it is the lows.

Our drive south was peaceful. Riley did well, although I had to climb in the back and nurse her a few times. We ended up in Baltimore, but Andy feared being so close to D.C. so we traveled further west to Frederick County, right by the West Virginia line. We checked into a hotel and planned to find an apartment the next day.

Life has a way of tripping you. Just when you think you're walking along to a better path, the road starts shaking and the earth cracks. You fall into a ditch and realize that you can't get out. Two options, sit in the ditch and complain the rest of your life. Or, sit in the ditch and tell yourself the view is quite beautiful.

I figured I'd spend my life telling myself, but never really believing, that the view is better from the depth of a canyon than it is from the height of a mountain.

I WOKE UP IN THE MIDDLE OF THE NIGHT TO THE HOTEL'S rattling heater. Riley slept beside the bed in a pack-n-play. Sweet, peaceful baby. I turned to Andy. Sweat covered his body. Again. I watched him sleep. Put my hand against his chest. His heart was racing. Really fast. He moved his hands. Eyes still closed. Looked like he was trying to button his shirt, only his shirt had no buttons.

I tapped his shoulder. He flung his body into a sitting position.

"Andy, you're doing weird things in your sleep. Are you okay?"

He exhaled. "Where are we?"

"In the hotel."

"I can't sleep. I just lay here all night. Every night." His speech was slow and slurred.

"You need to see a doctor. I think something's wrong."

"Nothing's wrong. I can't sleep, that's all."

"We're going to the doctor tomorrow, Andy. If you don't I am going to call the cops on you and tell them everything."

His head hit the pillow. "Where are we?"

"The hotel."

"Which state?"
"Maryland."

Chapter Twenty
Patrick

A week passed since I last spoke with Heidi. Hate to sound pathetic, but I caved in and went to her house. Still had my spare key, so I walked in when no one answered the door. House was clean. Wherever she went she didn't take much.

I saw an envelope addressed to me on the kitchen table. After smelling it, I opened it and read.

Dear Patrick,

I'm so sorry to have brought you into the mess of my life. There's so much more than I've shared. Andy made me promise not to tell a soul. I hope you can appreciate my desire to keep promises, no matter what it costs me.

I've realized some things, Pat. My time with you taught me a lot. You've shown me that the heart can live again after it stops beating. You've shown me that true love starts from the inside and works its way out. And more than anything ... you've shown me that two people can love each other mutually, more than they love their own selves.

I know my actions are hard to understand. Please know that I needed to leave and my love for you is part of the reason. You deserve happiness. You deserve better than me, Patrick. I know you would shake your head and say it's not true. What is true ... is that you're the sweetest guy I've ever known and it kills me that I may never know you again.

One day, after you've moved on and started a family with a beautiful wife, I will tell you why I had to do this. Right now just isn't the right time.

Please, let me go as you have let Emily go. Walk into your future with bright eyes and hope for tomorrow. There's hope even in the darkest corners. If I can say that, so can you. Find a way to live again. For me. For what could have been.

When you're ready ... if a nice girl walks into your life and gives you her heart, give her yours. Please.

I'm just a memory now.

Always in my heart,
Heidi

The letter was sweet, but it pissed me off. I ripped it up and left the pieces on her kitchen table, then walked out to my so-called bright future. I don't know what she intended, but the heart doesn't work like that. You don't fall in love with a person and swipe your heart back when it's convenient. The fact that she claimed she loved me, only to tell me that we couldn't be together and I needed to give my heart to another girl, seriously pissed me off.

What kind of sick game show did I end up on?

I left her house and tried to call her at the next stoplight, but her phone was disconnected. Not in service. She must've changed her number.

I punched my steering wheel, then squeezed it as hard as I could. I'm not an angry kind of guy. I don't pinch and hit and yell. I've never thrown anything across the room. But right then I sure as hell wanted to.

Not because of her. Whatever she did, she genuinely thought was for the best. I wasn't angry with her. Just the situation. The twisted circumstances that I never failed to shove my heart into.

I didn't say this often either, but I needed a drink.

Another email popped up on my phone.

From: Secret Admirer
To: Patrick Wheldon
Subject: Something you used to do...

Hey Patrick, just wondering ... what's one thing you did before marrying your wife that you wish you could do again?

From: Patrick Wheldon
To: Secret Admirer
Subject: RE: Something you used to do...

Hello nameless strange person, I used to skateboard. Haven't in years.

From: Secret Admirer
To: Patrick Wheldon
Subject: RE: Something you used to do...

Meet me at the skate park in 10?

From: Patrick Wheldon
To: Secret Admirer
Subject: RE: Something you used to do...

No.

From: Secret Admirer
To: Patrick Wheldon
Subject: RE: Something you used to do...

Okay. Well, maybe go by yourself? Might be fun to try it again. If you want company, I'll be spying on you from the tree branches. Watch out for flying acorns.

I laughed. Almost responded and told her that trees don't have acorns in winter, but I refrained. Never in a million years would I fall for a secret admirer, but curiosity lingered. Weird to imagine. Kinda creepy too. If she didn't know my friends, I definitely would've trashed her email.

Can't say the oddness of it didn't intrigue me though. Just a little.

Chapter Twenty-One
Heidi

ndy and I walked into an apartment building and he asked the lady at the front desk if we could see a vacant rental. She pressed a few buttons on the phone and a few minutes later a man walked up to us, shook our hands, and led us through a hallway, up two flights of stairs, down another hallway that smelled like curry, and to a door. He unlocked it, revealed the one-bedroom apartment with tan carpet and one small window by the kitchen, then asked us if we liked it. Andy looked at me. I nodded. I'd take anything at this point, didn't really care. Also liked that it was a month-to-month lease, just in case Andy left me again.

The man led us back down the hall, the steps, the other hall, and into the office. I signed a few papers. Andy refused to have anything in his name. He didn't want to be tracked. I didn't remind him that someone could probably find him through me if they really wanted to. Instead, I signed the papers, paid the deposit, and took the key.

"That easy?" I said.

The lady blew a bubble with her gum, then popped it. "Yup."

"Thanks."

We took our stuff out of the car and brought it to our new home. I set Riley's bed up in the bedroom and piled some sheets, blankets, and pillows on the floor beside it. Andy ran into the room, out of breath. What now? I wanted to say, but couldn't.

He reclined onto the pillows and stared at the ceiling.

"Andy, can I be straight up with you?" I sat beside him and pulled Riley toward me.

"Of course."

"If you leave me one more time you are never coming back. I will move on, get married again, and live as though you really are dead."

"But—"

"No."

"But if th—"

"I'm serious. If you leave me again I will never let you back into my life." I hugged Riley to my chest. "Or Riley's."

He extended his hand and we shook. Strange. Like a business deal or something. I hoped he understood my seriousness. No more fresh starts. No more games and fears ruling our lives. I couldn't stand it anymore.

He stood and surveyed our makeshift bed. "Probably be a little bit before we can afford furniture. Want to go get dinner somewhere?"

I bundled Riley in her winter gear and followed Andy back to the car. We drove around for a while, scoping out our new area for grocery stores, restaurants, and the nearest Target. I couldn't live without Target. Everything from bananas to underwear all in one place? Definitely a must-have in my book.

We settled on a local Ruby Tuesday's, ordered a three-course meal and talked about furniture in the midst of Andy's mild panic attacks. Every time his eyes snapped to-and-fro looking for someone out to get him I pictured Patrick. His peacefulness. The way he thought I was crazy for being scared of the dark. His strength. His lips.

I hated myself for thinking of him so much, but willpower didn't help. The heart can ignore the mind. Happens all the time. But the mind cannot ignore the heart. I tried, believe me. Doesn't work. The heart rules when the mind is in doubt.

"Do you see that?" He pointed to the decorations above our table.

I shook my head. Didn't see anything abnormal.

"They are everywhere," he said. "The Illuminati. It's a pyramid symbol. I see them everywhere I go."

"And that means?"

He leaned in and whispered, "They are watching us. See the eyeball in the pyramid?"

I rubbed my eyes, five times, hard.

"You don't believe anything I say."

"I don't know what to believe, but whether it's true or not, I don't really care."

"How can you not care?"

"I could get into my car right now, get hit by a drunk driver, and be dead. Why am I going to spend my last precious minutes of life worrying about how I could die, or how it might happen, or when it might happen? I'd rather live. When I die, I will die having lived, instead of living my last moments in fear of the end."

He tried to breath, his chest in a rapid rise and fall, like he just sat down after sprinting a mile. I reached for his hand, rubbed his knuckles, hoping my touch would bring him momentary peace. His hand tensed under mine until he pulled it away and waived the waitress to our table. She gave him the check, he paid immediately, then handed me the receipt.

"Read it," he said.

"What?"

"The amount of our bill."

"$66.60." I looked at him. "And?"

"It's 666, Heidi. Don't you see the connections? Don't you see the dots? Come on, please tell me you see it."

I tugged at my hair as heat blazed through my body. Rocking back and forth, I erupted and screamed so loud the people in the restaurant quieted and looked at our table. Dishes and forks stopped clanking. Waiters stopped filling drinks. I forced myself to sit as still as possible, clenched my fists, then screamed again. Once I got it out of my system, Andy ushered me out of the building. Riley cried the entire time. And we didn't say a word during the entire drive "home."

Chapter Twenty-Two
Patrick

Don't know why, but I decided to meet my secret admirer. Hilarious to even say that out loud. Why anyone would admire me, who knows. But someone did and she said she would only tell me her name in person.

I finally emailed and asked to meet her, but she said we needed to wait until I fell in love with her. Since that wouldn't be happening, I told her we could remain pen pals out of boredom. She agreed, but promised that one day I would marry her. The girl was nuts. At times I wondered if it was Miranda. She always seemed to flirt with me, subtle hints in her eyes, but she'd never do that to Heidi. Now that Heidi left, probably forever, maybe she thought she could find her way to me by playing this game.

Okay, so I kind of enjoyed it. But I couldn't tell if that was because I liked the attention and flattery, because I was bored and lonely, or because I genuinely found myself interested in this person. Our emails were always good. They ranged from flat-out strange and sarcastic to profound and intelligent. In other words, she had a brain and a sense of humor. I liked that.

But it was too soon to meet someone else. So I decided to keep the emails going. If I fell for her, then I would, but I wouldn't think about it in the process.

She convinced me to try skateboarding again. Why not? It had been almost ten years since I last touched my feet to a board. Didn't even own one anymore. So I bought a nice Zero deck and got everything else to put it together. Didn't take long before I pulled up to the empty skatepark at sunrise. Figured I'd skate before work. Mostly in case I looked ridiculous. At least then I'd be the only one watching. Well, me and my secret admirer. She asked for me to send her a video to prove that I did it. I told her I would if she gave me a clue to her identity. She agreed.

I practiced for a few minutes. Foot to board with the other grazing the asphalt. Once I got my bearings I tried some easy tricks, laughing along the way. The cold air refreshed me for once. Wind biting my face as I got comfortable enough to try a nose-slide again. I succeeded and glided my way to the vert ramp with a huge smile on my face. Nothing as freeing as skateboarding. I forgot how much I loved it. I set my phone on the top of the ramp so it would record as I skated. Then I went down the ramp and messed around. Even managed a three-sixty powerslide. So refreshing to ride again. Sometimes you don't realize how much you love something until it's gone.

Heidi's smile flickered in my mind. Dreams that die can live on in your heart, but dead dreams make dead hearts. I needed to live again. To feel life. Really enjoy it. To keep my heart alive and latch onto dreams that live forever.

If anything, my pen pal friend was a good distraction from Heidi. I hate to say it, but a good rebound. Sounds horrible, but sometimes it's true. Sometimes you just need to see that it's possible to love again before you allow yourself to move on. Otherwise you end up standing on the sidelines as the rest of the world skates by.

I sat on the ground with the board under my legs. Hit send on the video and got a response within minutes.

―――――――――――――

From: Secret Admirer
To: Patrick Wheldon
Subject: RE: skatepark vid

Wow! Lol. That is so funny. You look like you're really enjoying yourself. That made my day!! Thank you for really doing it. You look like a kid again.

Alright, so a deal is a deal. Clue #1 about my identity: my natural hair color is brown.

From: Patrick Wheldon
To: Secret Admirer
Subject: RE: skatepark vid

Natural color, huh? Is this Miranda? Are you messing with me or do you really "admire" me? Haha...

From: Secret Admirer
To: Patrick Wheldon
Subject: RE: skatepark vid

Not telling you who I am until you tell me you love me.

From: Patrick Wheldon
To: Secret Admirer
Subject: RE: skatepark vid

You may be waiting a lifetime then. Chances of me professing my love to a stranger via email are pretty slim. Especially with another girl on my mind.

From: Secret Admirer
To: Patrick Wheldon
Subject: RE: skatepark vid

You are the prize of my life and I'm going to win you.

Mark. My. Words.

I did mark her words, but not in a good way. I marked her down as a little over the coo-coo's nest, but for whatever reason I couldn't stop emailing her. All of our late night emails kept me company when I normally fell asleep alone. And during the day I liked having someone to laugh with. The girl definitely succeeded at making me laugh. Nothing like a woman with a sense of humor. I'd pick sense of humor over beauty any day. Yeah, I'd take humor over looks, but a sweet face would be nice to stare into as well.

Days passed and I found myself thinking about this girl in my dreams. During the day I couldn't wait to email her and at night I blinked at my ceiling wondering what she looked like, who she was, if I was given a third chance at this thing called love. They say the third time is a charm.

I went to my closet and pulled a bag from the back of the top shelf, hidden under layers of childhood memories. The bag crinkled as I pulled the box out and opened it. Sparkling in the nighttime glow, speaking of what could have been. Size 5. Ornate design. Three small diamonds and four baguettes. Would've been perfect on her finger.

I dreamed of proposing since the moment we first met. I wanted to wait until Riley's first surgery. I was going to propose right beforehand, telling her that I wanted to experience all life had to offer with her by my side, the highs and lows, the smiles and the tears, together. I hadn't decided on a method yet. Figured Matt could help me with ideas. His proposal was amazing.

Anyway, none of that mattered. I flipped on the television and picked up my phone.

From: Patrick Wheldon
To: Secret Admirer
Subject: What are you up to

Bored. What are you doing tonight?

From: Secret Admirer
To: Patrick Wheldon
Subject: RE: What are you up to

Thinking of you. If we have a boy first, what do you want to name him?

From: Patrick Wheldon
To: Secret Admirer
Subject: RE: What are you up to

Vanilla Ice.

From: Secret Admirer
To: Patrick Wheldon
Subject: RE: What are you up to

Wow! We are meant to be! That's exactly what I was thinking.

From: Patrick Wheldon
To: Secret Admirer
Subject: RE: What are you up to

I was thinking a lot today and I realized that I have spent the last few years "getting over" things. Dealing with life. Forcing myself to breath when I realize I'm so stressed that I forget to breathe normally.

When I was skateboarding (thank you for that) I felt that wind on my face and realized I was breathing again. I'm gonna be really honest with you because, well, because I don't know you and that makes this easier.

When I was a kid I was always the kid other boys came to when they needed advice. They'd ask me what to get their girlfriend on Valentine's Day. I was also the kid that never had a valentine. All the girls wanted to be my friend. They thought I was one of the girls or something because I was sensitive and paid attention to the needs of others. Anyway, I never dated much, but had a ton of girls who loved me like one of the girls.

When I met Emily she needed me. In a way the other girls didn't. She opened up to me in ways she never did for anyone else. She told me about the abuse she experienced as a kid and how she felt. Because of this, I became the one person who loved every part of her, not just the parts she showed people. So naturally she thought she loved me too, even though she never really did. She couldn't. I don't blame her.

Sorry to write a novel here. What I'm trying to say is that when I met this other girl, Heidi, I tried desperately not to fall in love with her. When I first saw her she was pregnant. What kind of guy falls in love with a pregnant girl? It was beyond her appearance. Something happened when we made eye contact. Then we became close. Once again another girl considered me her best friend. I was there for the birth of her baby. I was there when Riley rolled over the first time and got her first tooth. I was there. All the time. We were inseparable.

And something happened during those moments we spent together. Something changed in the way she looked at me. I knew she loved me. I knew it with every fiber of my being. And it was the first time I've ever felt that way in my life. Do you see what I'm saying? It was the first time in my life I looked at a woman, and she looked back at me, and we felt the same exact unexplainable love for each other.

That is true love.

And when you find it once, you want to fight like hell to keep it forever.

I like you. I think you're funny. Smart. Probably absolutely stunning. But you have a lot to live up to if you want me to fall in love again. It's only happened for me once and it was the highlight of my life.

There. Now that my heart is bleeding all over you.... Does any of that scare you away?

From: Secret Admirer
To: Patrick Wheldon
Subject: RE: What are you up to

Dearest Patrick,

Thank you for that...

No. It doesn't scare me away. All good things have to die one day. I have a history too. My past isn't the most pretty thing in the world. My parents never really loved me. I wasn't a boy. I tried to play baseball and football and hockey, meanwhile all the girls in my school were listening to the Backstreet Boys and trying to become figure skaters and horseback riders. Kinda funny, huh? You spent your life as one of the girls and I spent mine as one of the boys. Lol.

So yeah, I dated a ton of guys. Little opposite of you there. But I never gave my heart away. Not until this one guy walked into my life. He said all the right things, did all the right things, and so yeah, I fell for him. Looking back though I realize that I didn't really fall in love with him, I fell in love with the idea of him.

So fast forward through a bunch of hoopla and here I am.

I know you don't know me, but I'm asking you to give this a chance. We have our pasts. Okay. Lets throw them in the trash and move on.

If you just give me a chance to look into your eyes, just once, I bet it will be 5000 times better than what you experienced with Heidi.

So. Did I scare you away yet? If so, I was just kidding. If not, lets keep talking.

From: Patrick Wheldon
To: Secret Admirer
Subject: RE: What are you up to

This has got to be the craziest thing I've ever done in my life.

You are a true weirdo.

Now, time for bed. Talk to you tomorrow.

Goodnight nameless wonder.

Chapter Twenty-Three
Heidi

The next few days hummed by like meaningless scenes you fall asleep to during a movie. I drove back to Pennsylvania with Riley. Needed to meet my realtor, sign things, and go over stuff, then I came right back. Didn't even step foot in the house. Didn't want to. Ever again. Andy never left the apartment. I walked inside as he was carrying a piece of cardboard to the kitchen. He stopped, kissed my cheek, and kept going.

I stood in the empty living room as he duct-taped the cardboard to the window. Riley smiled as I bounced her on my hip. I tried to smile back. Tried to make her think life was normal. Everything was normal.

Everything was a disaster.

Andy clapped his hands together, pleased with his efforts, then turned to me. I raised my eyebrows, mouthed *ooookay*, and walked to the empty bedroom. Empty rooms galore. Andy didn't have a job, I didn't have a savings account, and no one knew my business in Maryland. My clients came to me via word-of-mouth and there wasn't any word spreading outside of Philly.

I promised myself I wouldn't cry anymore, especially not in front of Riley. Poor thing. She smiled her way through life, no idea that our world was making its way through a paper shredder. At least I had her. At least we had each other. And I'd never leave her. Never love myself more than I loved her.

Which made me wonder. Was Andy really the best thing for Riley? She needed a normal life. If I didn't homeschool her she'd eventually have to face her peers with a big weird contraption on her leg, She'd definitely get made fun of and feel different. I can only imagine how much more the kids would say if they knew her father was running from men in black who no one ever saw but himself.

She pulled on the side of her playpen and tried to stand. Looked more like a leaning tower. She smiled at me, chubby cheeks and all. I squeezed her cheeks and kissed her lips. "You have no idea, little one." She babbled and mumbled, then tried to take a step toward me. I grabbed one of her hands and placed my other hand under her short leg, trying to balance her so she could walk evenly. Her smile Windexed the cloudy sky and left no streaks, only blue as blue can be. For a few minutes I played with her on the floor, enjoying the sunshine, wishing it would last. I dreaded the surgeries and doctors and pain my baby would endure. Dreaded it more than I dreaded anything else. Soon she'd need me to have enough strength to blow her clouds away, and right now I barely had the strength to exhale.

Andy took a shower while I got Riley ready for bed, then placed her in her playpen and curled up on the floor beside her. A few minutes later Andy fell asleep beside me. I watched him. Couldn't sleep with all his jerky motions. Plus I felt horrible for him. His terrors haunted him even when he slept. My eyes closed and at some point my dreams took over. So vivid and detailed. A man and I holding hands as nurses wheeled Riley away for her surgery. He held me. I couldn't see his face, though I tried to make it out. My dream made him faceless. All I know is I felt at home in his arms.

I woke to Andy tapping my shoulder and whispering something. I sat up.

"Look what time it is," he said.

"3:33?"

"Another sign. They are messing with me, Heidi. They're playing mind games with me."

"Go to sleep, dear." I rubbed his head and ran my fingers through his hair until he closed his eyes. Never seen a soul so tortured. Made me want to take his place. Take it away and let him run free again. He needed a break from the madness. He needed a lighthouse to guide him back to shore. I watched him twitch in his sleep, wishing I could be a lighthouse for him, but I worried nothing would suffice. I worried the poor guy would die of paranoia.

Chapter Twenty-Four
Patrick

My ride to work changed from a warm car to a brisk ride on my board, and I couldn't have been happier. So glad Secret Admirer Chick told me to try it again. So many childhood joys get lost in the busyness of pretending to be an adult. I think Michael Jackson should've been admired more than he was. Well, maybe he was forced into his childlikeness because he never had the chance to be a kid, but still, I always admired his water balloon fights and afternoon tree climbs. People thought he was crazy, but he was just trying to find life inside of tragedy. Sometimes the only way to find life is to be like a kid. And skateboarding made me feel like a kid again. A recovered childhood dream that forced me to remember who I was before the storm. I was fun. And filled with life.

When I got to work I emailed her.

From: Patrick Wheldon
To: Secret Admirer
Subject: Childhood

What's one childhood joy you haven't experienced since you were a kid?

From: Secret Admirer
To: Patrick Wheldon
Subject: RE: Childhood

Mmmm... probably horseback riding. Did it once when I was ten, loved it so much it made me cry, but haven't done it since.

From: Patrick Wheldon
To: Secret Admirer
Subject: RE: Childhood

Go and do it. I have loved every minute of skateboarding. It makes me want to scream to the world... GO AND DO SOMETHING YOU LOVE RIGHT NOW! Something you haven't done in at least ten years. Then make the person next to you do the same thing.

From: Secret Admirer
To: Patrick Wheldon
Subject: RE: Childhood

Can I be super honest with you?

From: Patrick Wheldon
To: Secret Admirer
Subject: RE: Childhood

Yeah

From: Secret Admirer
To: Patrick Wheldon

Subject: RE: Childhood

Do you think we are just going to spend our lives emailing back and forth like this? Nothing happening? I'm thinking maybe we should stop. It doesn't feel right anymore.

From: Patrick Wheldon
To: Secret Admirer
Subject: RE: Childhood

What would it feel like if it felt right?

From: Secret Admirer
To: Patrick Wheldon
Subject: RE: Childhood

Like you wanted to meet me.

From: Patrick Wheldon
To: Secret Admirer
Subject: RE: Childhood

Maybe I do.

From: Secret Admirer
To: Patrick Wheldon

Subject: RE: Childhood

Maybe, but I'm starting to wonder if I can do this. I'm kinda nervous…
what if I'm doing the wrong thing? What if you regret this? What if I do?
What if life isn't meant to be as beautiful as our dreams?

From: Patrick Wheldon
To: Secret Admirer
Subject: RE: Childhood

I can't fall in love with you before we meet. I just can't give you that. I'm
up for meeting, but if you're looking for a husband, you're looking in the
wrong store. I'm not for sale. Not yet at least. And when I am for sale, if I
am, I will be a used and tattered heart, not a brand new one.

From: Secret Admirer
To: Patrick Wheldon
Subject: RE: Childhood

Okay.

She never sent an email after that. Neither did I. The "okay" distracted
me the rest of the day. I even called the cops thinking my car was stolen.
When they arrived they were pretty frustrated when I realized I rode my
skateboard to work, not my car.

Finally, I caved and wrote her an email, asking her to meet in person,
but I erased it. I don't know. My heart wanted to leap into an adventure,
but I couldn't give half of myself to someone. That's not me. I'm all in, or
all out. Completely understood Matt on that one. I didn't want to give her

any false hopes, so I let it go, deleted all of her emails, and skated home re-membering when I was sixteen and made girls sit in the backseat of my car so Dolly, my board, could ride in the front seat. Hilariously ironic. I decided to name my new board Folly. Seemed fitting.

Chapter Twenty-Five
Heidi

Took all I had, but I finally convinced Andy to go to the doctor. We parked in front of the hospital and he freaked out. Thankfully I drove. Otherwise he would've sped off. His hands quivered as I forced him out of the car. With Riley on my hip, I steadied Andy with my other hand. His pupils were tiny and he could barely walk to the entrance. Every step we'd take, he'd turn real fast, jerking his head, eyes darting all over the place, and ask me where we were.

We reached the entrance and he said it again.

"This is a hospital, Andy."

"It's a spy camp," he screamed, then charged off into the parking lot.

I jogged after him. Riley laughed. If only it were funny.

I found him hunched over by a row of bushes. "Andy, it's cold and I need to take Riley inside to change her. Please come inside. This isn't a spy camp. It's a hospital. You're not well."

"They're going to kill me if I go in there."

"Please come. You need to come. If they try to kill you at least we'll die together."

He limped to the door. I signed in and gave them his information. When I turned around he was gone.

A woman screamed. "Gun. Gun. Get down." Everyone in the room fell to the ground. Papers flew across desks and chairs toppled over. I panicked. He was right. Someone was going to kill us. And all this time I didn't believe him.

I covered Riley's ears and knelt on the ground with the rest of the waiting room. Then I looked up and saw him pointing a gun at everyone in the room.

Andy.

With a gun.

"Come near me and I'll shoot." He sounded drunk, but he couldn't have been. "I swear I will."

I stood and left Riley on the floor. "Andy."

A swarm of cops fled in and tackled him, pinning him to the ground. I ran to them. "No, no, he's my husband. They need to check him out. He isn't feeling well. Something's wrong."

They ignored me and took him away.

One of the cops stayed behind, "Mind coming with me, ma'am?"

I followed him through the wide eyes and toppled chairs, picked Riley back up, and hid my tears in her neck. My life was supposed to be filled with afternoon tea and cookies, late nights staring at the moon, and sunrises on the bay. Not this. Not anything close to this nightmare.

ANDY WAS TAKEN TO JAIL, BUT AFTER REALIZING HE WAS clearly unwell, they took him to a secluded room in a psych ward and strapped him to a bed. The doctor came out and ushered me back to his office. Riley and I sat in front of the desk. The chill in the air made me shiver.

He clasped his hands on top of a folder and cleared his throat. "This is a rare disease. Extremely rare. I can't know for sure until we run some tests, but he's showing all the signs and symptoms."

"What is it?" I said.

"Can you tell me how long he has been acting strange?"

"About a year, but he has a good reason for it."

"You don't understand, miss. He's dying."

"He seems fine. Just a little mentally unstable. I think it's stress. He had this job and everything starte—"

"No. This is a symptom of a bigger problem. I think Andy has Fatal Familial Insomnia. It's a rare condition. The simplest way I can explain it is that his body carries a gene. One day these people wake up and their lives change. It starts out with paranoia, strange phobias. This may last a few months until the panic attacks and hallucinations become more serious.

Eventually the patient experiences a severe case of insomnia. It may appear as though he's sleeping, maybe even sleep walking, but he's never really asleep. Not in a deep sleep, that is. It's a very serious and progressive disease. I'm afraid he is at the tail end of it, if my diagnosis is correct."

"I don't understand. He had this court case. People were upset with him. The fears were real. Some of them at least."

"He will die very soon." He fiddled with his folder, pushed around papers. "I'm sorry to tell you this. I know it's hard. His body will continue to fail him. His speech may change. These patients, they somewhat resemble dementia patients. Eventually they die. It's something you need to be aware of, however, because it may affect you again. Although it's not contagious, it is genetic." He looked at Riley. "At this time we have no cure or prevention. If your daughter carries this gene, she will inevitably experience the same thing."

I pinched my nose and held back tears. One person can only take so much before they lose all hope.

"It generally hits people between twenty-five and fifty years old," he said. "Although each case is unique."

"Nothing can be done? I don't understand. I've never heard of this. What is it doing to him? Is it like cancer?"

"It's a prion disorder which affects the nervous system."

"What does that mean?"

"It's a genetic mutation. The patient loses his ability to sleep and this degenerates the body and leads to death."

I stared at him. Blinking. Wondering. Waiting for an end to the nightmare that had become my life, but he only stared back, in silence, conveying to me the truth of my reality, the truth that all things, whether or not we want them to happen or not, will happen the way they are meant to. Life goes on. Hills of happiness and valleys of despair. It's all there. And I wasn't sure I could do it anymore.

Sometimes I could handle the hard truth, the realities that made the average person want to crawl into a hole and die. For the last year I handled Andy's disappearances and odd secrets, wondering whether he was crazy or really being chased and followed by some gang related to a bank scandal. It made sense. He really testified in court. He really had people bothering him.

They even put graffiti on our house one day. For so long he allowed himself to fall victim to anxiety over the court case and it messed with his mind and made him believe people were out to get him. And sometimes I believed him. Brief moments here and there, I believed him. Really thought some insane people were after us. I saw black cars in front of my house all the time. Weird stuff. Men following me. Maybe it was all in my head, because apparently a lot of it was all in Andy's head.

But all this time, all these days without him, he was dying. His body degenerating by the second, without him knowing. The poor thing suffered and didn't even know what was going on. He believed whatever truths the hallucinations played in his mind. All the while, I was falling in love with another man.

I hated myself for it. One-hundred percent hated myself for it.

Chapter Twenty-Six
Patrick

You ever notice how single life is so different from "taken" life? When you're heart is set on someone else you go to the grocery store and ignore all the other girls. You see a container of orange juice and think of breakfast with your girl. You see apples and think of the time you sat under the apple tree. Everything reminds you of that person. And if it doesn't, you find a way to make it remind you of her. Then, you're single. And everything you see makes you feel like crap, so much that you desperately want to start new memories with a new person, just to erase the others. Before other girls were invisible, but now I walked through the grocery store and saw every curve of every woman. From the petite blonde near the potatoes to the tall brunette by the cereal. Suddenly every woman became a potential eraser of past memories.

I couldn't bring myself to meet my secret admirer girl. Maybe because of the pressure. She said from day one that we would be great together, soul-mates with unfathomable passion. That's asking for failure. It sets up too much tension and takes away everything natural about falling in love. So, when I saw the cute little redhead standing by the bottled water, I asked her to go on a date with me.

She crinkled her nose, looked me up and down, and put her sparkly engagement ring an inch from my eyeball. Embarrassed, and half annoyed at myself, I walked away and emailed Secret Admirer from the checkout line, then erased it again.

Maybe what I missed most was my friend. Heidi and I were never more than friends. Not even sure how I knew I loved her. All I knew is living without her was worse than dying.

Enough of Heidi.

Enough of it all.

For once, I wanted to kiss something other than my pillow on Valentine's Day. Is that so much to ask?

NORA CALLED AND ASKED ME IF SHE COULD COME VISIT again. She'd be in the area for an audition in New York and wanted to take a road trip so she could stop by Philly. When she arrived I hugged her and tried not to inhale too much of her sweet smell. A woman's smell has the power to intoxicate a man, and I wasn't in the mood for intoxication.

"Did you want to meet up with Miranda?" she said. "She just texted me and I'd like to see her before I leave tomorrow. I know it's been a long drive and I'll probably hang out with you guys more on the way back, but I need to do something right now. Car rides make me think too much. I need to not think."

I shrugged. She pointed to my car, so we got in and drove to Miranda's, picked her up, and drove to a local diner. Everyone ordered. The girls talked while I sat there, the man in the middle, the man disguised as a girl. One of the ladies. The best friend guy. They guy no one ever falls in love with because he's too nice. Made me want to do something bad. To flip out and slam someone across the table, demanding some horrible meaningless sex. Just to say, "Hey, I'm still a dude. I do, in fact, have a penis."

Nora stopped talking and looked at me. "What are you laughing at?"

Did I laugh out loud? I laughed again. "Nothing."

"Are you having conversations inside of your head?" Miranda asked. "You know they have meds for that."

She did that thing women do when they flirt. You know, when they blink their eyes slowly as they grin. Head tilted just so, one finger touching the rim of her drink.

"Are you flirting with me?" I said, mocking her as I smiled and rubbed my glass. "Sure seems like it."

She flipped her bright hair behind her shoulder and laughed. Nora laughed too. And they both waited for me to say something else. I tapped the table and pointed to Nora. "What about your love life? Anything going on there?"

"I've got someone," she said, looking down. "Not sure how it will work out. He's into someone else. I don't know. Taking it slow. Waiting for him to lead."

"What's he like?" Miranda said.

She looked at me. "Kind of like you."

Miranda looked at me.

"What's everyone looking at me for? I'm just the teddy bear girls like to hold when they're lonely, but shove aside when the big sexy man comes along to save the day."

"No," Miranda said. "You don't give yourself enough credit. You're a great guy. You deserve someone special. So, what do you want in a girl?"

"I don't have a list."

"Not even a few qualities?" Nora said.

"No qualities. No hair color preferred. No height. No ideal bra or butt size. No specific hobbies or interests."

"Then what do you want? How do you know when you find someone worth dating?"

"Chemistry."

"As in biology, chemistry, physics?" Miranda said. "My favorite subjects ever."

"As in … laughter, tears, smiles. Everything feels right with her. I can't explain it. The world just stops. Everything freezes. It's me. It's her. It's just us. Everything else, every molecule, including the oxygen we breathe, is only secondary to the chemistry we create. When we watch a movie it's more than images strung together in the form of mindless entertainment. It's an experience. An experience we share together from making the popcorn to watching the film to talking about it for days after. Chemistry. What more can I say? You either have it or you don't."

They stared at me, eyes wide, jaws almost to the table. I guess the teddy bear could pull some romance out after all. Hidden underneath heaps of mud-slathered unrequited love. The teddy bear is a real man! I laughed again.

Miranda shook her head. "And people say I'm weird."

Chapter Twenty-Seven
Heidi

The doctor officially diagnosed Andy with Fatal Familial Insomnia. That didn't stop Andy from his paranoia though. He believed a gang still wanted to kill him. Maybe this is a little crazy, but I went along with it to make him feel better.

After sleeping in the apartment for the fifth night I asked the doctor if there was any way we could move Andy to Pennsylvania. "I'm sorry," he said. "The drive would be too much for him and sometimes they can be dangerous at this stage. You remember the incident at the hospital. That is not unlike these patients. Many of them are restrained in their last days. I'd say he is doing better than most I've treated. Moving him at this point would be really difficult though, especially that far away."

I walked into his room and stopped. Stared at him. Strapped to a hospital bed in a white-washed room with terrible lighting. The final moments of his life spent in a bland room with beeping machines and no family or friends. I begged him to let me tell his parents, but he said not to. I called them anyway, against his wishes, but his mother didn't believe me, said I was nuts, and threatened to take custody of Riley if I didn't get my act together, so I apologized and hung up, wishing I never tried to call.

I touched his hand. His eyes flickered.

"Andy?" I said. "I've got Riley here."

"You shouldn't be here. They will kill you."

"I snuck past them in a disguise. They won't kill me."

"It's hard for me to talk. I'm losing my voice."

"I can tell."

"I think they are poisoning me."

"I will try to get you out of here. Until then, I will keep sneaking in." I

137

kissed his fingers. "I want to thank you for rescuing me and trying to save me." A tear fell. "And for keeping me safe from the bad guys. You're a good husband. You've done a good job. I'm proud of you."

"I'm dying, bug." His eyes were swollen shut. "They are putting poison in my food and forcing me to eat it."

"I know. It's okay though. You are a strong man. They may be able to kill your body, but they can't kill your spirit."

"Bug."

"Yeah?"

"We took our rings off because I wanted to put them back on when it was new." He gasped for air and tilted his head back.

I stood. "Are you okay?"

I almost called for help, but he settled back down and looked into my eyes, then closed them again. "Find a good man, Heidi. Not just for you. Riley needs a father. You are young. I want you to find someone. It doesn't upset me. You need to move on and live your life. Please do it for Riley. Promise me."

"Andy."

"Promise me."

"If it happens, it happens. If it doesn't, it doesn't."

"I can't sleep. It's terrible. They keep coming in here with guns. They point them in my face and scream at me. It's not easy. I almost wish they'd kill me already."

"I will try to save you. Maybe we can run away from here and go to the Bahamas. I will go buy the plane tickets now."

He nodded. Life slowly drained from his body. I could almost see it happening as his pale face lost the pink tint it once had.

"Rest here while I get the plane tickets. When I come back I will wheel you out of here."

I let Riley kiss him goodbye, very much aware that it could be the last time, but it wasn't. Later that day I came back and sat beside him.

"Andy," I said. "We're in the Bahamas. Isn't it beautiful?"

A slight smile.

"I'm going to take Riley down to the water. You stay here and relax in the sand."

He tried to nod.

A few seconds later I said, "She loves it here. I was thinking we could come back once a year." I held his hand. "The water is crystal clear. Sky is so beautiful too. You can barely tell where the sky ends and the water starts. I love the fish. Tons of them. All around. Mmm . . . can you smell that? There's nothing like that salty beach smell. Maybe we could go snorkeling later. For now, how about we relax here and enjoy the silence?"

I found a recording on YouTube with sounds of waves crashing against the shore. A few weeks passed. I did the same thing every time I visited him. Then, on a snowy February morning, two days before Valentine's Day, I played the beach sounds for 42 minutes until Andy slipped into a peaceful coma. Or at least I hoped it was peaceful.

The doctor assured me that Andy could still hear me. Probably even understand me. But he couldn't open his eyes or speak to me.

I sat there. Staring at his face. Void of life. Waiting for the end. Every time I left him I thought it was goodbye, but a few days passed and he was still there. Lifeless, but breathing.

I couldn't cry. Andy died to me the first time he left, when he made me believe he was involved with a scandal and needed to fake his death. Seeing his body there, relaxed and lifeless, the reality I lived for months became real. I didn't have to lie anymore. Soon, he would be gone. Permanently. Never to arise from the shadows again.

I kissed his forehead and smiled, then took Riley outside for a little and came back in. About an hour later he stopped breathing. With Riley asleep on my shoulder, I rubbed his hand as his face twitched and relaxed along with every muscle in his body. Riley woke and I leaned her toward his face. "Kiss daddy goodbye, love." She pressed her lips into his cheek and I helped her wave. "Goodbye, sweet Andy. No more suffering. It's all over now."

I DROVE BACK TO PENNSYLVANIA AFTER ANDY'S DEATH AND arranged to have him cremated, like he wanted when he faked his death before. I debated whether I should tell his parents the truth after my call with them, and decided not to. Figured it would be too heartbreaking for them to know the suffering he endured. Not to mention grieving the loss of your child twice seemed unbearable. Doubt they would believe me anyway. Since the day I "stole" Andy from his mother she barely spoke to me. Not an ounce of love for me in their hearts. For some reason it never bothered me much. I was used to it. Never had many friends growing up and was never good enough for my parents either.

I set up a time to meet with my realtor, paid some bills, and settled back into life without Andy. Only this time I knew he'd never come back. I searched the house for any small remnants of him that Riley would want when she grew up. After putting everything in a box I sat on my bed with the photograph Andy gave me for Christmas. The night I sang him the song I wrote for my future husband.

Strange how memories can fade so much into the past that it almost seems like another life. I loved Andy. I really did. But the person I was back then wasn't me anymore. She died when he left the first time, and now she was really buried. For good.

I didn't know who I was anymore.

Riley cried from her room. Nap time over. I picked her up, "My little lady bug. How are you?"

I set her on the ground with some toys and watched her play, hoping I wouldn't watch her die the same way Andy did. Didn't think I could bear something like that twice.

All that time in Maryland by Andy's side and Riley's birthday snuck by me. We had a mini celebration at the hotel, but nothing much. Already a one-year-old. Time flies. Most one-year-old babies I saw were walking or starting to walk. Not Riley. Only one foot reached the ground. A few more months until her surgery. The first of many. I dreaded it with every part of me.

I texted Miranda. *Want to celebrate Riley's first birthday tomorrow?*

Miranda: *Whoa. You're back? New phone number? I thought you were gone forever.*

Me: *I'm back. Please don't tell Patrick. I'm not ready to see him yet.*

Miranda: *He has a secret admirer.*

Me: *He does? Well, good, then he doesn't need me anymore. Don't tell him I'm back though. I need time.*

Miranda: *Where'd you go?*

Me: *A break. Meet me at the park by my house tomorrow. We can sing happy birthday to her there.*

Miranda: *You don't care that he has a secret admirer?*

Miranda: *Nope. Thanks for telling me though.*

Me: *You sure you don't care?*

Miranda: *Never been so sure in my life.*

My eyes glazed over when I saw the shredded paper on my kitchen table. Patrick read my letter. Read it and ripped it up. My words must have meant nothing to him. Not when my actions were so strange. How could I expect him to take it well? I broke his heart. I needed to tell him the truth soon, but not yet. Not until my life felt somewhat normal again. I needed to sell the house, start over, and develop a new life that didn't feel like a bad dream. And I needed to do it asap.

Chapter Twenty-Eight
Patrick

C all it boredom, call it attraction, call it crazy, I don't know what caused me to email her again, but I did. A simple, "Hey, how's it going?" And within a half hour she responded. I kicked my feet up on my couch and read her words.

From: Secret Admirer
To: Patrick Wheldon
Subject: RE: Still there?

Hey Patrick,

I'm so glad you emailed again. I've been thinking about you. Listen, I want you to know that I found someone else. I think about you and wonder if what we could have had would've been wonderful, but you didn't seem ready. Your heart isn't here. It's with Heidi. Trust me, I respect that. I really do. I've found a good guy and I want you to know that it won't hurt my feelings if we stay friends. That's all we can be now.

My heart did a three-sixty right inside my chest. Would've flipped right out and landed across the room if I didn't sit down. Women entered and left my life at lightening speeds. I couldn't keep up. Not sure I wanted to anymore, but as I reread her email a second time one thing stood out to me.

She found someone else, but maybe, just maybe, judging by her tone, she'd give me one more chance.

From: Patrick Wheldon
To: Secret Admirer
Subject: RE: Still there

Nameless wonder, I'm sorry I dropped off the face of the planet. I'm sorry for a lot of things I can't help. I'm not a perfect person, and okay, so I'm not looking for a perfect person either. I know you found some great guy who probably deserves you more than I do, but when I read your email the first word that came to my mind was "shit!" I didn't know I'd regret losing whatever strange relationship we had until you said that. This could be the unimaginable loneliness talking. It could be the brink of spring in the air and my friends all happily in relationships. I don't know what it is, but right now I'm feeling an immense loss and sense of regret when I think of you finding someone else. Can he wait? Is it serious? Can we meet one time before you devote yourself to him for the rest of your life?

I hit send and waited. An entire hour and fourteen minutes. I cleaned my kitchen, vacuumed the floor, took a shower, counted sheep, and finally she responded.

From: Secret Admirer
To: Patrick Wheldon
Subject: RE: Still there?

I'm really sorry. I don't know. I'm afraid you're just saying that because you don't want to lose another friend. We can still be friends, but if I meet you

I want to marry you. Period. You have to choose before we meet.
From: Patrick Wheldon
To: Secret Admirer
Subject: RE: Still there

I have to choose right now? Or we can keep talking a few more weeks and see how it goes?

From: Secret Admirer
To: Patrick Wheldon
Subject: RE: Still there?

April 1st. You need to make a decision by April 1st. If you still want to meet at that point, we'll meet on the condition that you must marry me whether you are attracted to me or not. If you don't want to meet at that point I will never speak to you again. Deal?

From: Patrick Wheldon
To: Secret Admirer
Subject: RE: Still there

Deal

Chapter Twenty-Nine
Heidi

A few weeks of hard work in the coldest month of the year, at least to me, and I finally moved out of my house into a smaller apartment. Two bedrooms. Enough for Riley and me. That's all we needed. It felt so good to walk away from that house. Not that I wanted to forget Andy, but I wanted to forget the house. Everything went downhill in that house. Way down the hill. Way down the hill and into a canyon.

I lost so much of myself within those walls. So much of what I wished I could've been. My dreams of a happy family with a happy baby. Instead, I lived a nightmare with Andy that I believed was real, only to find out he couldn't decipher reality from fiction anymore. He died, really died this time, and my heart beat inside the container I now gripped. The urn filled with his ashes. Closure. Real closure.

I needed to do one last thing before I talked with Patrick. I needed to say goodbye to Andy and spread my old bruised heart across the earth along with his ashes.

Miranda watched Riley while I drove around Pennsylvania to every place Andy ever spoke about. I started with the house he grew up in. Pulled along the side of the road, watched birds flutter from branch to branch, and tossed a handful of his life into the air, then drove away to the next place.

The place he had his first real kiss. The movie theatre at age fourteen. I drove behind the building with the window down and the cool air on my face. Breathing it in, I scattered another handful of him into the world he once loved.

Hand out the window, I kept going and pulled up to his favorite place to unwind. The Susquehanna River near the big old bridge that joined one county to another. I got out of my car, sat under the bridge, and imagined

Andy sitting in the same spot years before. A lonely college student looking for purpose. For love. His thinking place, as he called it. Little did he know . . . his life would be cut short. Too soon. Before he had a chance to really live.

I reached my hand into the urn and stood, tossing him into the river along with my former dreams. The ashes swirled in the air and settled in the water. I wiped the rest of him from my hand, shed a single tear, and walked back to the car. Using my iPhone I turned on his favorite music. The Beatles, Elvis, and anything before 1960. I listened as I drove to the place we met, let more of him slip through my fingers, and moved on to the garden we married in.

Behind a charming Victorian bed & breakfast, we set up rows of chairs and married in a beautiful oasis filled with every color and scent imaginable. I stood in the place we said our vows, his ashes tucked under my arm, and our wedding rings in my pocket. So much hope stood in that very place years earlier. The way he looked into my eyes before he kissed his bride. The way my knees buckled with anticipation and worldly dreams. Romance, at the time, meant passionate sex, breakfast in bed, and looking at each other with longing every second of every day. I looked forward to our life together. Our life as Prince Charming and Cinderella, only to be fooled into the reality of bills and jobs and crushed dreams.

Romance meant more to me now. More than laughter and longing. I couldn't explain it. Romance, true romance, killed my childish dreams and replaced them with something real. Something of significance. Deeper and darker and brighter all at the same time.

Faithfulness. Gentleness. Patience. Goodness. Kindness. Peace. Joy.

Love.

True love.

I dug my finger into the earth in the place I once vowed to remain faithful to the man I loved, until death parted us. Then I placed our rings inside, mingled with dirt and tears and the last of Andy's ashes. The earth, fresh with spring mist, would soon make room for new life. Like my heart. Before I covered the ashes and rings with more dirt, I planted a tiny seed. A seed that would wrap its roots around our rings and blossom into something beautiful.

"Andy," I said to the ground. "We've been through a lot. I stayed faithful to you for so long. Did everything as you wished. We were young, had difficult times. A strange life most people couldn't fathom experiencing. Now, death has parted us, for real, and I've learned a lot. You've taught me that real love is more than good feelings and butterflies in the stomach. It's faithfulness even when it's painful. Joy even when you want to cry. And patience when you want to scream. It's the opposite of everything negative and the wholeness of everything positive. You've taught me this, Andy. And now that death has parted us, I'm burying this old, tired heart with you, and hoping that when the life I once lived dies and this seed brings a beautiful flower into the world, that I will have a new heart to give to someone else, and that you will be happy for him." On my knees, I sobbed, clenching the dirt with my hands. No matter how much you want to bury something from your past, it still hurts to let go of a part of you. I caught my breath and stood. "The life I now live is different than the one I lived with you, but I promise to never forget what we shared. You were good to me and I will make sure Riley never forgets that. Thank you, dear Andy." I waited for the ground to respond, but it didn't.

Empty urn in my hand, I walked away. Imagining a little red wagon with a little white bow. My dreams. I poured the last of them into the earth and hoped, with all of my heart, that the seed would grow and flourish into a simple, sweet flower.

I ALMOST DROVE AWAY FROM THE COUNTY ANDY GREW UP IN, but I realized I had a few ashes left in the urn and although I'd probably regret it, I really wanted to stop by and tell his mother the truth. By the time I parked in front of their house I almost turned back around. When Andy was alive we only visited them a few times. Every visit ended in an argument and Andy and I fled the house as his father yelled from the porch. They had yet to meet Riley. His mother couldn't bring herself to visit at my place and, I don't know, maybe it's wrong of me, but I felt like she needed to get over herself if she wanted to meet her grandchild.

My gaze swept over the pristine garden. Not a weed in sight. And the finely swept porch and sparkling bench on the porch. His mother prided herself on being clean. Always said "cleanliness is next to godliness," but I didn't see the connection. Cleanliness, to that degree, seemed more like a mental death sentence. She valued a dust-free home more than her own children, refusing to visit Andy or his brothers because their wives didn't keep the house clean enough. I once asked her if she'd come and visit us if we stayed outside, but she refused.

I walked up to the door, stood there a few minutes, and walked back down the steps.

A man's voice blasted through the quiet air. I turned. Saw no one at the door.

"You stupid excuse of a woman," the man yelled. "What did I tell you? I like my dinner warm, not hot." Something crashed and shattered. Sounded like glass against a wall. I tip-toed down the steps and the door opened.

I turned. Andy's father. He looked me up and down, smirked, revealing half of his yellowed-teeth, then stepped out onto the porch. I inhaled, deep and slow, then started to speak. He waved his hand, quieting my attempt, and rested his hands on his belt.

"Look who finally decided to show up," he said. "What? Do you need money?"

I handed him the urn. "This is what's left of your son. He had a rare genetic disease which you probably have as well."

"Don't tell me what I have or don't have." He clanked his teeth together. "You and your stories. Maybe it's time to live in reality."

"Andy had a genetic condition which caus—"

"I haven't cared about Andy since the day he left this house. His last words to me were enough to write him off forever." He backed up, closer to the door. "So as you can see, I could care less about you and that deformed child of yours too."

"She's not deformed."

"Sure as hell seems like it to me. Crippled. Deformed. Retarded. Which word do you prefer?"

I walked back to my car as he slammed the front door and disappeared behind angry walls. I put my keys in the ignition, but his mother showed up at my passengers window, motioning for me to open the window as she looked behind her to the house. I unlocked the door. She sat down and looked in the backseat.

"Riley's not here," I said. "I just spread Andy's ashes across the county and had some leftover." I motioned to the urn between our seats. "Thought you may want them."

A tear settled on her nose. She tried to speak, but couldn't.

"Andy had a genetic disease. He suffered a mental breakdown of sorts. Believed he was being chased by people and I believed it for a while too. What I said when I called you was true."

She looked back to the house, then whispered, "He tells me what to say. He controls everything I do. I'm not allowed to like you because you are a part of Andy. He hates Andy." She spoke so fast that every word blended into the last. I could barely understand her. "He hated Andy since the day I gave birth to him." Her chest shook as she placed her hand over her heart. "Andy is another man's child. I cheated on my husband and got pregnant with Andy. He knew it wasn't his baby because he stopped having sex with me after I had the children. He liked prostitutes better."

I thought for a minute. The air between us cold with a cryptic silence. She surveyed my face as I did the same to her. The front door opened. He stood on the porch, flushed with a poisonous madness. I cringed.

"Mrs. Chase," I said. "I'd better get going."

She squeezed my arm and leaned closer to my face. "I'm sorry for the way I've treated you. When you live with a critical heart it's easy to become that way yourself. I know the way I've been isn't right. I hated you because you took Andy away from me. Andy was the closest thing to me. The only person I ever bared my soul to. Closer to me than my own husband." Her hands shook as she opened the door. "Please don't feel sorry for me. I've hurt a lot of people in my life. I deserve every second of the way I'm treated."

She walked back into her home. I considered calling the cops, but feared what would happen to Riley if I meddled with their lives. I drove away as Andy's childhood house disappeared. I tried not to cry, but the tears came anyway. I judged her so fiercely. Her hate for made me never want to be around her. For so long I believed she despised me because of my dust-bunnies and the papers scattered in my car. She ridiculed and picked me

151

apart from the first day I met her, from my height to my occupation. Now it made sense. She had attached herself to her son, unhealthily so, because of the absent love in her marriage.

Life is never as it seems, I thought as I wiped my face with my sleeve.

Love can make people do crazy things, but the absence of love can make people do even crazier things.

I felt sorry for her.

WEEKS PASSED. COULDN'T GET MRS. CHASE OUT OF MY HEAD, so I started writing her letters. She never responded, but I faithfully mailed one every Friday in hopes that she received at least one of them. Didn't know what to expect, but hoped she'd be a little encouraged to know that someone knew her pain and felt sorry for her. I'm not a big fan of pitying people. Pity seems to make things worse, but sometimes a little pity can make someone feel less alone. Plus, I felt horrible about the way I judged her and wanted to do whatever I could to love her instead.

Life changes so much. One blink and you're twenty with the world at your fingertips. The next blink and you're almost thirty with the world falling apart around you. By the time I'm forty, I thought, maybe life will be normal.

I imagined my future life. Would I be married again? Would I have more children? Would I be happy?

A picture of Patrick's face flashed in the back of my heart. I pulled it to the front and dwelt there, missing his eyes, his touch, his friendship. After all this time, after all I did to him, would he open his heart to me again? Could he? Was it even possible for us to start over?

I needed to see him again. One more time.

Even if he didn't love me anymore, he deserved the truth.

Chapter Thirty
Patrick

Beautiful spring afternoon. Saturday. A few friends and I had a cookout at Gavin and Ella's. They planted an amazing garden over his grandparents graves, at the request of his late grandfather, and wanted to show it off. Really they needed an excuse to have a get together.

The girls sat in the shade under a few trees. Ella's pregnancy was really starting to show. The very beginning. Meanwhile Lydia looked like she could barely go another day before giving birth.

Tylissa moved in with Gavin and Ella. The house was huge so it worked out well for them. Just to give her some time to get on her feet. Mwenye would most likely never come back.

I walked to the deck and sat between Matt and Gavin. Reese sat across from me.

"Did you invite James?" I said to Gavin.

"Of course. He's bringing Abby over later. They had a birthday party for a cousin or something."

"How's Sarah?" Reese said.

"She's doing okay," Gavin said. "A lot of pain, but she's handling it well. It's almost a year since it happened. She'll be home soon."

"Wonder when they'll get married," Matt said.

"When she's ready. That's what James said. Will probably take some time." Gavin shook his head. "Can't imagine."

"I hate to burst everyone's bubble of depressing conversations," I said. "But I have something positive to add to the table."

Gavin and Matt raised their eyebrows.

"Are you serious?" Matt said.

"Maybe this sounds like the most ridiculous thing in the world," I said.

"But I love her."

"Have you even talked on the phone yet?" Matt said.

Gavin smiled. "I can completely relate."

"So at least one person doesn't think I'm crazy," I said.

Reese smiled. "Good for you, man."

"Don't you need some kind of closure with Heidi first?" Matt said.

"No. She wrote me a letter before she left. I know it's over."

"Miranda said she came back months ago," Matt said "You two never talked?"

"Negative," I said. "She let go. And I need to respect that."

"So, you love this new girl?" Matt said. "Hate to sound skeptical, but you haven't officially ended things with Heidi and you are already in love with a secret admirer? What if she wasn't at my house that night? What if it's some Internet stalker who follows you on Facebook and never knew any of us? Even worse, what if it's really some creepy old man?"

Gavin laughed. "Matt, we all know you have the gift of skepticism. Let the guy live. I bet it will work out just like it did for Ella and me."

Matt tilted his chair on its back legs and exhaled. "Suit yourself. I think it's strange, that's all."

"What do you expect?" I said. "She told me we couldn't be together. Ever. She left. Then she came back and didn't say a word to me. Yeah, I gave her everything in me, but this new girl—"

"Do you even know her name?" Matt interrupted.

"No. She doesn't want to tell me until we meet in person. Anyway, she's helped me live again. We have a lot in common. Our conversations are amazing. I mean, some of the deepest conversations I've had in my life. I really feel like we would be good together. I can't know until I see her in person, but I'm finally ready. She told me we could meet in person when I fell in love with her. I think I might be."

"You think you might be?" Matt said. "Poor Heidi."

I slammed my drink on the table. A few birds flew from a branch above us. Gavin put his palms on the table and stood. Matt shrugged and rubbed his face.

"You both need to calm down," Gavin said. "Let the guy live his life the way he wants. He's the only person who needs to agree with his decisions."

"Do you agree?" I said to Gavin.

"Doesn't matter what I think," he said. "But yeah, she sounds nice. Meet her and see how it goes. If it's a disaster then consider finding Heidi and talking again."

"Heidi is done with me."

"How do you know?"

"Miranda told her I have a secret admirer and she said she didn't care. So Miranda asked if she was sure and her response, and I quote, 'Never been so sure in my life.'"

Gavin looked at Matt. And Matt looked at me. "Okay," he said. "I'm sorry. I'll admit I was wrong. But only this once."

"No problem, man. I know you're just looking out for me."

I COULDN'T WAIT TO GET HOME AND EMAIL HER. WE DEVELoped a nightly routine, somehow fell right into it. Every night around 9p.m. we emailed each other and talked about our day. Not the boring stuff like grocery shopping and tying our shoes. The good stuff. The heart stuff.

Emily and I never talked like that. She vented. I listened. Heidi never vented. She never talked much about Andy or her problems. I didn't talk much either. We had a comfortable silence that resonated with both of us. More than anything, I think her and I were sent to each other because we needed peace during that time. We needed a break. An eye in the midst of the storm. Sadly, we weren't meant for anything more.

It took me a while to come to terms with it, but the more I emailed mystery woman, the more I realized I had to let Heidi go. Matt tried to convince me to shoot for the happily ever after, but I reminded him that my "ever after" is plenty happy, it's just not what I expected it would be. And that's okay. It doesn't mean I settled for less. It doesn't mean I gave up on something that could have been beautiful. What it does mean is that I came to terms with reality and gave room for a new one to form. Or so I thought. I needed to meet her to find out.

And so, I emailed her at 9:14p.m.

Marilyn Grey

From: Patrick Wheldon
To: Secret Admirer
Subject: You can't know until you know

Alright miss nameless wonder, I have a story for you. Once upon a time there was a boy. Silly, stupid boy. He spent his entire life alone, wandering about, kicking gravel, tossing rocks into the water. Waiting. For a girl to wander about, kick gravel, and toss rocks into the water with him.

Girls came. They went. They came. And well, you guessed it, they went.

Silly, stupid boy gave his heart away, not easily, but he did. But there was never a girl silly and stupid enough to give him her heart. So he almost gave up completely on girls, thinking they must all be too serious and smart for someone as stupid and silly as him. Then, some weird, silly, stupid girl walked—sorry, typed—into this life.

She may have been a creepy old man, or a prank played by friends, but he realized one day that he wasn't happy until they talked—uh, typed.

He realized, you see, that he was stupid enough to fall in love with a woman he never saw with his eyes, but that's okay, my dear, because the heart doesn't need eyes to fall in love.

So, I'm ready to know you. To know your name. To touch you. To, dare I say it, kiss you.

If you'll have me....

Skate park. Tomorrow. Sunset.

I stared at the email on my iPad, my finger hovering above the "send" button, the button that could instantly change my life. And would. Because I hit send and exhaled. A weight lifted. A huge weight I'd been lugging around for years. It lifted and vanished. I choked up, squeezed my forehead, and let one tear loose. A memory from elementary school appeared in my mind. The smell of crayons and construction paper. Glue smeared on my fingers. My teacher helping me wash my hands. The pretty girl next to me who needed her hands washed too. I let her go first. As much as I hated glue on my hands. My teacher smiled and said, "You'll be a good husband one day." I've made it my goal since that day to be a good man, a man worthy of a good wife. And perhaps, for once, I was about to fall in love with someone who loved me as much as I loved her.

I leaned against the headboard of my bed and waited what seemed like an eternity.

I couldn't sleep. At all. The entire night. Finally at 8a.m. I fell asleep and didn't wake up until the afternoon. As soon as I got out of bed I checked my email from my phone. Nothing. What if I made the wrong decision? What if Heidi really was the one?

I glanced at the engagement ring on my nightstand, picked it up, and almost regretted my email yesterday, but I thought of Heidi's words. She cared about me, a lot, but she didn't love me the way a wife should love her husband, she loved me the way a best friend loves her best friend. Sorry, but I wasn't interested in best friends anymore. I wanted a wife. My heart couldn't handle the chase anymore. I wanted to stop running after women and sit down with one, sip lemonade, and enjoy life together.

So, I got myself ready, chewed on some mint gum, and drove around until about an hour before the sun would set. My stomach twisted up in knots when I parked. One other car. Had to be hers. I checked my reflection in the window of the car, then looked toward the skate park. Not a person in sight.

I looked around the park, careful not to look stupid, but saw no one. I waited an hour, skated around, sat in the middle of the park, skated more. Nothing. The sun started to hide its warmth from this side of the world as all of my hope left with it. She never showed up.

I called Miranda.

"Hey," she said. "What's up?"

"Are you guys playing a prank on me? This isn't funny."

"What are you talking about?"

"You know what I'm talking about."

"Your secret admirer?" She laughed.

"It's not funny. I'm seriously getting pissed now."

"I talked to Heidi," she said.

I blinked at the glowing sky, wondering if I wanted to know what she was about to say next. A heart can only take so much rejection.

"She's doing good," Miranda's voice cut through the desired silence. "She said she is ready to tell you what happened soon, but she wants to make sure you know that you can't be together. She's been through a lot and she's not ready for that yet. But," she said. "I do know who your secret admirer is and let's just say this . . . she will be there tonight. She left my house five minutes ago. Don't worry. She's coming. Just a little notorious for being late."

"Who is it? Nora?"

"I can't say."

"Is it Nora?"

"If it was Nora would you be happy?"

I hung up the phone and almost cried. I didn't feel that spark with Nora. I didn't know if I could. Last thing I wanted to do was break another person's heart. Only one option. I needed to leave before she arrived. Maybe face her later. I didn't have the energy to crush her dreams. I guess I was hoping it was someone altogether new. Not Nora. Not Miranda. Just something new. Something good.

I stood in the middle of the ramps and rails, saturated in the hues of the golden sun. I looked to the West. Pinks, purples, blues, oranges. A surreal sky, like something out of Photoshop. Then it caught my eye. A single rose on top of an envelope in the middle of the park.

I knelt down, picked it up, and scanned the surroundings. Still no sign of Nora. So I opened the letter and read.

Dearest Patrick,

Did you really think I'd let you get away? The first time I saw you I knew you were something special. I'll never forget the first time our eyes locked across the room. Before we had our first conversation I knew we were meant to be, and it scared me, everything about it scared me. I wasn't ready. I didn't expect it. Naturally, it made me want to run, but I couldn't. Something pulled me to you and I haven't been able to stop thinking about you since that first day.

So maybe you'll understand why I had to take the secret admirer approach. There was no other way for us to be together. Not with your heartbreak. Not with my issues. So I figured we could keep in touch this way. Get to know each other in a different way. Maybe then you'd understand how much I love you, how much I need you more than I've ever needed anything in my life.

Patrick, I've been waiting so long to say this. It's killed me. I've wanted to tell you how I've felt, but the timing was never right.

It's right now.

Some love stories don't make sense, so let's not try to make sense of this.

Sweet Patrick, you are my life. I can't wait to be yours. I'm nervous. It feels like the start of my life. And to think . . . all this time we've been best friends too. Falling in love inside out.

I love you. I love you. I love you.

Confused, I stood and looked around. In the soft light of the sunset, I saw her standing by the gate. Arms at her sides. White shirt hanging off one shoulder. Skateboard at her feet. I squinted. Paralyzed, I couldn't move closer to see her. To find out if I made the right decision. She didn't move either. I wanted to run in the opposite direction.

But I took a step, trying to calm the butterflies in my stomach from flipping out. Until I saw her eyes. Then I knew.

I could no longer control myself as I flipped out along with my insides. I shook my head. "Am I dreaming?"

She shook her head. Tears. All over her face. Her beautiful, precious face.

"How?" I said, inching closer. "It was you the entire time?"

She nodded. "Pat, I'm so sorry. I'm so, so sorry for everything."

I fell to the ground, kissed her feet, kissed her ankles, tried my hardest not to cry. She grazed my head with her hand, then tugged my hair and forced me to look at her.

"I love you," she said, then knelt on the ground in front of me and looked through my eyes, to that place inside a man only the right woman can find. "I gave you my heart a long time ago, Pat. I needed to take care of some things and I feared losing you. So I created this secret admirer. It was all an act. I needed to talk to you, but the timing wasn't right for us to be together. I'll explain everything soon, but just know that I lov—"

"Stop, Heidi. Just stop. I don't think I can handle all of this." I held back tears and coughed. "Is this real? Am I dreaming?"

Our fingers locked. She closed her eyes and I finally let a few tears go. Still kneeling on the ground, my hand linked with hers, I touched her face with my other hand. Took in every feature from the fullness of her lips to the way her cheekbones highlighted her eyes.

"You're everything I've ever wanted and so much more," I said as I ran my fingers down to her lips and held them there. "I thought I'd never see you again." She opened her eyes. The pink and orange sky reflected in them. For a few minutes we stared at each other in silence, her hands enveloped in mine. I wasn't sure if she wanted me to kiss her. After all we went through, I didn't want to offend her, but I couldn't take it anymore. The way she looked at me, through me, like I was a mirror of her very self, an extension of her very soul, made me want to burst into flames so we could melt into one.

I wanted her to be mine. Only mine. For the rest of eternity.

I moved my face closer to hers, then moved back and looked down. Saw the rise and fall of her chest. Her breathing, rapid yet drawn out, proving the passion between us was about to explode.

I grabbed the back of her neck with both hands and pulled her into me. She collapsed in my arms, face pressed into my neck. The softness of her lips lingered on my skin, half-open with her breath sending waves of electricity down my body. Heat pulsed through me, shocking every part of my tired heart from its slumber. We squeezed each other until we could barely breathe, then she pulled back and started to talk, but I moved toward her mouth, tossed my hat to the ground, and steadied myself centimeters from the lips I'd been dying to kiss for so long.

I feared the beginning of our first real kiss, knowing within minutes it would be over. So I stayed there, our breath heavy and slow, mingling with each others in the lavender-scented air. I took it all in. Her lips, begging for mine. Her eyes, gently closed in anticipation. A dogwood tree shedding its white flowers around us. The sun, now rising on the other side of the ocean, offering us a final ray of amber light before saying farewell. Butterflies danced around my stomach, desperate for an opportunity to fly.

I took the opportunity. There, in the sweet passion between us, our lips touched. And touched. And touched. We said goodbye to our history and hello to a new life together. Our paths finally crossed, and with this one action, this one amazing kiss, I knew the two paths would never diverge again. I'd see a thousand more sunsets in her eyes.

Together.

It felt so right. To love. And be loved. All in the same moment.

We stood back. Laughed. Cried. And hugged again and again. The butterflies left us, fluttering up past the trees, somewhere else, to land inside another person longing for love. Another love story to ignite.

We stared at each other under the stars, still on the pavement at the skatepark, reveling in the aftermath of our first kiss, and knowing that there would be so much more to come.

Life never felt so good.

Chapter Thirty-One
Heidi

Days turned into weeks and I swear I felt more in love with him every other millisecond. I told him what happened to Andy, how I finally let go, and how horrible and guilty I felt for falling in love with him while still married. I gave him the full truth and it felt so good to release every chain shackled to my heart. Patrick understood. He sympathized. Encouraged me. And told me he'd help me through everything else in life. Never again would I be alone. He almost made me forget about Riley's first surgery, but sure enough the day had come. We packed everything for a trip to Baltimore. Pat took off work to come along.

We arrived the night before and unpacked our stuff in a nearby hotel. After putting Riley to sleep I curled up on Patrick's chest. He swept his hands up and down my arm, finally resting on my hand.

"You okay?" he whispered.

I pressed my fingertips to his. "I'm scared."

"She will be okay."

I shook my head. "I'm scared of a lot of things. Of her being put to sleep, of life getting too complicated, of myself. What if I'm making the wrong decision? What if she suffers too much and would have wished I had her leg amputated instead?" I sat up and looked at his concerned eyes. "What if I fail her? What if I can't do this?"

"I wanted to wait."

"Wait?"

"I didn't want to do this right now. I wanted to wait. Make it special. Romantic."

"What are you talking about?"

"Some love stories don't make sense. They don't top the best sellers

163

lists or become classics. People don't rave about them. They are the three star reviews. Neither here nor there. They don't go over the top, but they don't go under either."

I laughed and kissed his cheek. "What are you talking about?"

"Well, you see, some love stories don't have a thousand rose petals and pianos in the middle of nowhere to set the mood. They have a dingy hotel room with a sleeping baby about to endure hardships. But it doesn't matter, right? Because the beauty is inside of us. You and me. Who we are together." He reached into his pocket. "So I don't need all that five star shnazz to ask you to be my wife." He held a box in front of me, then opened it to reveal a sparkly ring. "Heidi, I bought this ring a long time ago. We've been through so much and I thought I'd never get to ask you this." He knelt down on the bed. I sat cross-legged in front of him with an enormous smile on my face.

"Will you be the woman to make me the happiest husband in the world every day for the rest of my life? Will you walk this road with me, even—no, especially—when it gets hard? Will you smile at me every morning for the rest of your life, no matter what happens?" His smile brightened the dim room. "Be my wife, Heidi. Forever."

I couldn't speak. Couldn't cry either. Not even happy years. It was like my happiness reached so high that it surpassed even the joyous tears that normally come on occasions like these. I could only stare back at him, nodding my head and smiling. He slipped the ring on my finger. Beautiful ring, almost looked vintage, but I didn't notice details. I wanted to look back at him instead.

"Thank you for loving me," he said, hiding his tears behind a laugh. "You're the first girl to really love me, all of me."

"Same to you, Pat." I wrapped my arms around his neck. "I've never experienced anything like this before. It feels so uncanny, to have such a mutual connection. I still can't believe it."

He held my face. "Listen to me, we are a team. Everything you face in this life . . . I will be with you. None of that self-sufficient mess anymore, we're together in everything. Don't try to hold in your pain anymore. If you're feeling sad, come to me. If you're frustrated with me about something, tell me. If you're happy, smile with me. Okay? I need you and you need me. This is the start of our life together." He kissed me, still holding my face. "And it's going to be amazing."

THE DOCTOR EXPLAINED SOME THINGS TO US AS PATRICK LIS-tened. I tried to, but failed. Riley rested her head against my shoulder as I swayed by the window, shaking. They allowed me to take her to the operating room, but Pat needed to stay behind. I got dressed in the clothes they gave me so I wouldn't carry germs to the room, then waited and dreaded putting her to sleep. They gave me the breathing mask to put over her face to induce her sleepiness. A wave of pain crashed against my heart as my babies eyes struggled to stay awake. Her little face staring up at me with no idea about surgeries and pain and machines.

In a little while they would cut her body open and fix her crooked leg. Hurt me almost as much as it would hurt her. Trembling, I willed myself not to cry until Riley fell asleep.

Then her eyes closed and her body went limp.

Through tear-laden eyes I saw the nurse urge me to leave, but I couldn't. I couldn't let my baby go.

"This is too hard," I said.

The nurse held my arm, but didn't say a word.

After a minute, she finally said, "Sweetheart, it's for the best. Just think, after she heals she will be able to wear a shoe lift on that foot and finally walk and run."

I kissed my little girl, wetting her cheeks with my tears. A thousand men could break my heart, but it would never compare to the pain I felt for my daughter.

Escorted by a kind nurse, I left my sweet little love bug and met Pat in the waiting room.

I looked at him and immediately burst into tears. "You were the only one with me when she was born, and now you're the only one here as I say goodbye to her for the longest amount of time I've ever been away from her. The two hardest days of my life."

He wrapped his arms around me and pulled me into his chest. The feeling of being wrapped in the man you adore. No comfort better than that. I took a deep breath and motioned toward the seats in the waiting area. We sat down and he pulled a bunch of things out of our bag.

"What's this?" I said.

"Well," he said, handing me a large book. "I can't take credit for this. It was Ella's idea, but I thought it was a good one." He pulled a stack of papers from a bag. "I figured you wouldn't want to leave the waiting room while she was in surgery, so I thought it would be nice to do something fun. I also wanted it to be memorable, so Ella told me to buy a bunch of craft stuff and we could create a memory book for Riley. We can start at the beginning and leave room for our future together." He looked into my eyes. "The future of our family. Then once a year we can come back to it and make a page together. The three of us."

I smiled and laughed. "Is she the queen of romance or what?"

"Pretty sure they beat us all. They are a five star romance." He laughed. "And this will be nice, but I still like our three star story better."

"Well, maybe most of the world would give our story three stars, but I'd give it ten."

He squeezed my hand and looked at my ring. "I still can't believe you're going to be my wife."

"I still can't believe it either." I admired the ring. "Do you believe in soul-mates?"

"I believe in you and me."

"But if one person is meant for us, then were our previous relationships a mistake? Was it pointless?"

He thought for a minute, then looked so deep into my eyes I thought I'd pass out. His love for me could turn a stark hospital waiting room into an elegant garden. And it did. Right then. His eyes punched holes in my heart only to pour in love and close it back up. I caught my breath and looked down.

"Heidi." He touched my face with such gentleness. "Maybe it's not one person. Maybe the tale of soul-mates was put into the world to make people discontent with what they have so they buy more stuff to fill the void. Who knows. All I know is that it doesn't matter. We put our entire selves into our marriages before, and we barely got anything back. Not saying that's what love is about, but now we have something mutual. For the first time in my whole damn life I can look into a girls eyes and find her looking right back at me. Not passed me. Not around me. Into me. We are so good together. The world can call us secondhand love all they want, but I never prided myself on following the world anyway. You are what I want. Soul-mates? Yes. We are. I know it when we look at each other. Is there more than one soul-mate for each person? Doubt it. Can you marry the wrong one? Probably. I don't know the answers to life's most treasured questions. But there's no doubt in my mind that what we have is right."

A tear warmed my cheek as the dust around us shimmered in the bands of light. I touched his hand and brought it to my lips. Our eyes met again as I kissed his fingers. Electricity emanated between us. Enough to light the entire hospital. I smiled. He smiled. *You are right,* I said to him with my eyes. *We are so good together.*

An old man tapped my shoulder. "Ma'am."

I turned toward him. Patrick leaned over my shoulder.

"I'm here for my grandsons surgery and couldn't help but overhear your conversation." He smiled and leaned forward onto his cane. "When I was a boy I met a girl and just about gave my life to be with her. Pretty young girl. Great personality." He cleared his throat. "But she left me for another man. Got bored with me, I suppose." He laughed. "I was at the local market one day. It was 1952. In walks this girl wearing an ugly sweater and glasses bigger than her head. I didn't think much about her until she left the store. It was like someone turned the lights off and closed the shop. The sun disappeared at noon. I found her outside and asked her to go to lunch with me. We've been together since that day."

"Wow," I said.

"So you think you married the wrong person first?" Pat said.

"Not at all." He grinned so bright you could see the little boy in his eyes. "I married the right person. She taught me how to love. Without her and her unfaithfulness I wouldn't have learned the value of being faithful. So she left me and another one enters my life. There's no wrong or right when it comes to love. It's like you said, when two people are so wrapped up together that they can't remember whose dreams are whose, then it's better than right. It's divine."

I smiled. "Whose dreams are whose?"

"Oh, you know, when the ballet princess goes to the baseball game. When the football star goes to the opera. Simple love. When you stop having 'his' and 'hers' and instead you have 'ours.'"

Patrick kissed my shoulder and smelled my hair. I leaned into him and allowed the man to disappear, then the room, then my past, then myself. Lost in him, in our love, in the beauty of surpassing *right* and *wrong*, I kissed his cheek, held my lips there, and embraced the *divine*.

Never, in all my life, did the sun shine so bright in my life. My dearest, sweetest, most precious friend. My Patrick. My love. My everything.

"Truly," he said. "You complete me."

Rebelling against a life of black and white, **Miranda Ryan** paints the world in a technicolor fever. She spends her free time on park benches, analyzing people from the outside in and creating whimsical stories about their lives. Unbridled and full of life, her ever-changing heart is a revolving door no man can figure out. And she likes it that way. But when Derek Rhodes enters her life, he stubbornly challenges her every move. As she unsuccessfully avoids this opinionated prankster her colors fade to gray and she is forced into a choice . . . to lose *the self she knows* or *the self she has never been.*

Derek Rhodes wears the same shade of brown every day and avoids eye contact with strangers, until Miranda walks into his life and splashes his world with streaks of colors he swore he'd never touch. Drawn to her imaginative personality, he finds himself questioning his own cynical nature and flat-lined ideals, only to fall in love and realize the only woman he's ever let into his heart has no plans of letting a man into hers. Follow them both as they poke and prod and test each others limits on a journey of discovery.

Out by Valentine's Day 2014

Chapter One
Heart on a Shoestring
Miranda

Some people spend their lives walking by people on benches, while others spend their lives sitting on benches analyzing the people who walk by. My friends would say I'm the one racing by the lonely bench sitters, candy pink hair tossed in the wind, dreams clutched in my shoulder bag, stars in my eyes, but I'm not.

I know, it's shocking.

Once again, streetlights twinkled in the April air as I sat on another iron park bench. The best place on earth. At least to me. The place where people became stories and stories became dreams and dreams sparked the hidden echoes of my heart. All on a paint-chipped park bench.

An older woman jogged by and stepped on someone's lost newspaper, crumpling it and sending it flopping down the path behind her. One persons hard work, another's doormat. I turned my head and watched her jog into the clouds, back to her smiling newborn and eager husband, back to the beauty of her family.

She passed a young couple huddled together, shivering in the nighttime chill. They walked by me, laughing, her head tilted back against his chest, eyes on the budding tree branches above them, their love story unfolding like a handwritten note from a seventh grade crush. Excitement abounds. His arm, tight around her waist, and the frown on his face when she checked her phone, showed his possessiveness. But the cherry lipstick mark an inch from the corner of his mouth showed that she liked being owned as much as he liked owning her.

I listened. Watched. Breathed in and adored all that lived around me. Around me. Always around me. I so envied the world around me. Don't get me wrong, I loved my own life too, but that didn't stop me from wishing I could close my eyes and slip into someone else's life. You know, explore the world with different eyes, a different heart.

Another couple walked by, swinging hands in the breeze. A ring sparkled on her left hand, but not his. Engaged. Judging by their excitement he proposed recently. He looked ahead as they passed me. Her eyes met mine, then she turned to make sure he wasn't looking at me too. Funny. Her insecurity would sure enough wilt their relationship. Odd considering her preoccupation with herself seemed more important than him. Her awkward five inch heels and layers of makeup made it obvious. When he tried to touch her hair she pulled back and rearranged it. Perhaps she had mistaken the eyes of lust for the beat of his heart. They walked into a growing fire. Soon their swinging hands would fall to their sides as she consumed herself with dresses and flowers and cakes. Everything but her beloved. The beginning of the end. The end of their bliss. The beginning of struggles and conflicts and maybe, just maybe, their love would triumph through it all.

Rare though.

I'm not cynical, I swear. You can call the sky blue or you can find a way to make yourself believe it's green, but in the end it's still blue. I'm not afraid to see blue even when it's not the most appealing. Love is hard. It's not easy to make love to a person only to find out that their very person is chipping away the rotted parts of your person, making you into something better, but often in the most excruciating ways. That's when most people run. But hey, that's love. Becoming one. Being one. Living as one and morphing your soul into the soul of another.

A group of high school kids walked by. Joking and stepping on each others shoe laces while slapping gum and spraying out a colorful array of cuss words like graffiti on the walls of life. Heads held high, shoulders back. Maybe juniors. Just on the brink of saying goodbye to their senior friends and claiming the role themselves. The ever coveted senior status. When you think you're the coolest thing to walk the locker-lined halls, when really you're just like everyone else. A puppet in the game of life. Controlled by everything around you and not enough inside you.

I stood and walked away from the bench, becoming a passer by. I nodded to each empty bench I passed, bowed, said hello, and kept walking. Not hello to imaginary friends. Sorry, I'm not that weird. Saying hello to the dreamer that would sit there next, wishing and hoping to slip into the life of a passerby for a minute. Only a minute. To see if the grass is really greener on the other side.

I walked fast, tilted my head back, and stretched out my arms. Couldn't hide my smile if I wanted to. The cool air clung to my cheeks as the stars twinkled above. Enormous fire balls that never moved. Ah, what it would be like to be a huge ball of plasma. So neutral. Yet so exhilaratingly beautiful, held together by your own gravity. Yes, gravity. Stability. Words I had yet to acquaint myself with. I coalesced with no one. Not even myself.

I looked ahead. Dreaming of the day I'd share these thoughts with another soul. It would take a lot for someone to know me. The real me. Not even sure if I did.

Love. It would be hard. Very hard. Breaking down my walls and letting someone in? I don't know. I liked my life. Singleness didn't scare me as much as marriage did. Commitment. Falling in love a thousand times appealed to me more than falling in love once and working to feel in love with that same person every morning and night of my life. For. Ever.

Besides, most guys were far, far too normal for me. And I just can't do normal.

"Oh, are you a southern belle tonight?" a man said.

I turned. Ah, Earl. The skinny homeless man with one half of his dirty button-down shirt tucked in, just like his life. He dreamed to help the world, to do something nobel prize worthy. He always spoke of Rosa Parks and Maya Angelou. But his breath always smelled of Jack Daniels and he could barely help himself off the curb. I scooted my dress out of the way, did a curtsy, and said with my finest southern drawl, "Fancy seeing you here tonight, Mr. Earl. Need some help off thissy here curb?"

He nodded and took my hand. I helped him to the park bench where he leaned back and almost passed out.

"Yesterday you were Irish with blue hair and now you're a southern lady with a huge dress and pink hair," he said. "Unless you are a dream."

"Why, yes, sir. My name is Annabelle and we're back quite a few decades in the state of Georgia." I spun in a circle. "Would you like to see my five step waltz?"

"Your five step what?" He mumbled and smiled. "You about the strangest girl I know."

"My pleasure." I bowed and danced away, down the streets of life, right to my apartment door.

Derek called me, but I ignored and skipped up the steps and unlocked my door. He wanted to visit again. He was nice and all. Extremely attractive, in a rugged Johnny Depp kind of way. But strange. And boring. Nothing like his sister, Ella, who saw life through the eyes of Cupid. And I dreamed of a man who would dress up with me and dance the streets of Philadelphia. He barely changed his shirt, much less his mind. I couldn't even convince him to ride a go-kart.

Not my flavor starburst, that's for sure. I wanted a cherry. A little sweet, a little sour, and yum-diddly-licious. He was a lemon. Yellow, but not like the sun. More like a bitter, rotten lemon rind. Did I mention that he was nice though? He was nice. And had a great smile. A great smile he rarely showed.

He texted. I ignored and rolled onto my bed. Feet in the air, hoop dress a flying, I smiled.

Life didn't need a man to be enjoyed. In fact, for me, a man could ruin everything. Take my fun and leave me lifeless.

Mmm, yeah, not ready for such things. Not ready at all.

Chapter Two
Heart on a Shoestring
Derek

No one, and I mean no one, pissed me off like Miranda did. She flirted like someone playing darts with no hand-eye coordination. Not a lick of aim in her body. A casual flirt who probably gave hundreds of guys the wrong impression, like she obviously did to me, but something drew me to her. No idea why. I swore off women long ago. Marriage? Not for me. That didn't change, but I couldn't help myself. I wanted to see her again. Her odd and dimpled smile and whacked out hair styles. If anything, just to laugh.

I needed to laugh. Work zapped the life out of me like a squirrel eating an electric wire. My parents convinced my sister and I to go to college. Ella lasted a week. I lasted eight years. Yes. Eight. Don't ask.

Eight years of school and all I had to show for it was a dingy apartment and faded jeans.

Derek Rhodes. Marketing Manager for Doodle Dandy Dog Candy. At your service. Pleased to meet you. How do you like my fake smile? Good. Great. Wonderful.

The only person I can blame is myself. No one, not even my parents, knew my successes or failures. I told no one who I was and what I really did. Even created a fake name and legally changed it. My family knew me as Derek Rhodes. My old colleagues knew me as David Bennett. I kept the two world's separate. No one could know David Bennett. I didn't even want to know him. Hated everything he did and loathed that I became him.

Yeah. Needed a smile.

Something to take my mind off of what could have been and help me start over. But the girl wouldn't answer her phone. Only when she was bored. According to her I was too normal and only wanted as a last resort.

Not like I wanted to get into her pants, just wanted a friend.

Thirty-three years old and spending my life at Doodle Dandy Dog Candy didn't exactly provide the most friendships. And the friends I did have were all married and sprinkled across America. Kids. White picket fences. Minivans. The whole eight-and-a-half yards of normalcy.

Miranda could say I was normal all she wanted, but I didn't have kids, a white picket fence, and certainly no minivan. Couldn't fathom driving one of those ghastly things.

A text popped up on my phone screen. Miranda finally responded. *What's going on tonight Mr. Rhodes? Counting the tiles in your ceiling again?*

You are so annoying, I typed back, then erased, and typed, *If you think I'm so boring how about answering your phone so I can live a little?*

Miranda: *Impossible. I've tried. You are not receptive to my ingenious plans.*

Me: *I'm coming up this weekend and I will be at your house Saturday at noon. If you want to hang out... be there.*

Miranda: *Is the glass half full or half empty?*

Me: *The glass is a figment of your imagination. See ya Saturday.*

I couldn't figure out if she was genuinely an annoying person or if the age difference made her seem immature. Especially the hair. I can understand dying your hair every so often, but almost every week? And I'm not talking brown or blonde. I'm talking rainbow bright.

Immature, annoying, either way she made me laugh and shake my head. And I needed a break this weekend anyway.

AFTER AN EXHAUSTING DRIVE TO PHILLY, I STOOD IN FRONT of her apartment door, caught my breath, and knocked. A few seconds passed, the door knob wiggled, and the door jerked open to reveal a grinning Princess Leia. A grinning Princess Leia with pink hair.

"What the hell are you wearing?" I said. "I thought we were going out to eat?"

"What? You don't like?" she said in a hushed Princess Leia tone. "Let's walk the town and pretend we're fighting evil."

"Seriously, Miranda." I shook my head. "Change your clothes. Is that *Moonage Daydream* playing in the background?"

"I'm not changing. You need to change." She pulled the edge of my sleeve. "Brown, brown, brown. Every time I see you. Do you own anything else?" She tugged my hair. "And do you ever wash your hair? I'm all about the Kurt Cobain look if you can make it appealing, but this ain't appealing buddy."

I turned and walked away. Fast and agitated. She yelled from the doorway. "Don't be so boring. Live a little."

I got in my car, slammed the door, and stared off before starting it. Why did I let her frustrate me so much? Her opinions didn't matter. Boring is relative. To an introvert a party with a big group of people is boring. To an extrovert a calm afternoon at the bookstore is boring. I'm not freaking boring, I convinced myself. She didn't even know me. How could she judge who I am based off my shirt choices and lack of desire for roller coasters?

"I'll show her how ridiculous this is," I said to myself, then started the car and made my way to the mall. Took a while to find everything I needed. Once I did, I changed and drove back to her apartment, and threw rocks at her window until she appeared in the doorway, still Princess Leia. I hid from her view, then flapped into sight, light saber glowing in the evening air as I twisted it and turned around as though fighting some invisible person. "Come down, Leia. I am the force. And I am with you."

She covered her mouth with her hands and laughed, then jumped up and down like someone who won the lottery. I waved her down. She held up her hand, ran inside, and returned with her purse and keys.

"Miracle of all miracles," she said, smiling way too much. "No guy has ever dressed up like Han Solo for me."

"No guy ever will again. Seriously, you realize how dumb this is, right?"

"It's fun. And I think you look kinda good like that."

I laughed. "You do this for some kind of validation. It's not normal. If you were truly confident in who you were you wouldn't need to change all the time."

She rolled her eyes and walked back to the steps. I grabbed her arm and forced her to look at me. "See," I said. "You run from what I'm saying because it's true. You don't want to face the person you are so you avoid her by being all these other people."

She jerked her arm from me and stomped up the stairs, making it a point to slam the door as loud as possible. And me. Alone. At the bottom of the steps, wishing I didn't have to be so opinionated. Or at least didn't speak my opinions so much. David Bennett spoke his opinions and everyone loved him. But everyone hated Derek Rhodes whenever he spoke up.

Still. I was right.

Out Valentine's Day 2014

Pre-Order on Amazon Today!

Your Questions Answered

Q. Why did you have to make Sarah get burned? I feel so bad for her!

A. Sarah is a strong character and very beautiful. She fought cancer and won. She is hard to break and she needed to be broken. There's pain inside of her that could only be opened in the most dreadful circumstances, but in Book #5 *Bloom* you will see her blossom into something even more beautiful and I can't wait to share her story with you.

Q. Is Sarah's story based on anyone in real life?

A. Yes, every character I write about it based off of something or someone I've seen before. Sarah's story is realistic and gritty, but oh so beautiful too.

Q. Was it hard for you to write Heidi & Patrick since your ideals are more in line with Ella?

A. A little. I'm Ella through and through, so writing about two people falling in love after being married once isn't natural for me. I'm definitely a "one person is it" kind of girl, but people change and my ideals have been challenged, just like Ella. I've had to look at love from different angles and realize they are all just as valid as any other. Just as beautiful in their own way. As unique as the people in love. It was hard at some points to write Heidi & Patrick, but these people come alive on the page and if I don't let them do and say what they would do and say, they'll end up all the same. Little replicas of me. So I need to let them grow and be who they are.

Q. What's the deal with Mwenye? Is he really innocent?

A. You'll find out in Book #6 *A Starless Midnight*. This book will be different than the others. Of course the romance will still be there. The beauty. But it will play out a little darker. There are political undertones in this one. It deals a lot with racism and true justice. Something I'm really passionate about.

Q. So there will be a book for Nora and Myra too?

A. Yes! You'll get to read their stories in their own books. We've listed the order on my website for anyone interested.

Q. How can I get free books? I'm obsessed with this series!

A. Apply for my street team. Details are on my website!

Q. Have you fallen in love yet yourself?

A. It's a secret, but my heart is set on someone special right now. :)

Q. Will you start another series after this?

A. Yes. I'm tossing around ideas right now. It's like creating a new world after I say goodbye to this one. I need to pick a setting, find the right people, and develop the story from there. I enjoy writing smaller books that link together as part of one huge story, so I think I will definitely start another one after this. Stay tuned for more updates by signing up for my newsletter!

If you have any questions you'd like to see answered in the next book, please email them to Marilyn at marilyn@marilyn-grey.com and we'll select some to answer. You will also receive an answer from her via email. She adores her fans and responds to every email she receives.

Do you love The Unspoken Series?

Don't forget to connect with Marilyn on
Facebook, Twitter, and GoodReads. She is so excited
to hear from fans and talk about the characters
in *The Unspoken Series* with everyone!

www.ingramcontent.com/pod-product-compliance
Lightning Source LLC
Chambersburg PA
CBHW021043130626
46552CB00005B/1994